INVENTING THE REAL

The 2X2 Series

General Editor: Florence Howe

The Riddle of Life and Death
Tillie Olsen and Leo Tolstoy

Here and Somewhere Else
Grace Paley and Robert Nichols

The Power of Weakness
Ding Ling and Lu Hsun

To Stir the Heart
Bessie Head and Ngugi wa Thiong'o

Rites of Compassion
Willa Cather and Gustave Flaubert

INVENTING THE REAL

—

EDITH WHARTON AND
HENRY JAMES

WITH AN INTRODUCTION BY
MARY ANN CAWS

The Feminist Press
at The City University of New York
New York

Published in 2008 by The Feminist Press at The City University of New York, The Graduate Center, 365 Fifth Avenue, Suite 5406, New York, NY 10016

Library of Congress Cataloging-in-Publication Data

Inventing the real / Edith Wharton and Henry James ; with an introduction by Mary Ann Caws.
    p. cm. — (2x2 series)
  ISBN 978-1-55861-576-2 (pbk.)
 1. American fiction. I. Wharton, Edith, 1862-1937. Old maid. II. James, Henry, 1843-1916. Real thing.
  PS645.I58 2008
  813.008—dc22

                        2007033832

Text and cover design by Lisa Force
Printed in Canada

13 12 11 10 09 08   5 4 3 2 1

CONTENTS

—

Introduction by Mary Ann Caws   I

EDITH WHARTON

The Old Maid   I5

HENRY JAMES

The Real Thing   II5

INTRODUCTION: VERSIONS OF THE REAL

—

Edith Wharton (1862–1937) and Henry James (1843–1916) met first in Venice in the late 1880s, when she was in her late twenties and he in his forties. They were American writers who could not have known that they were to be paired and compared, if not during their lifetimes, then long afterward. They were introduced by a friend of both their distinguished families, and, on their next meeting, as Wharton writes in her autobiography, *A Backward Glance*, she chose to wear a designer dress and a new hat in order to appeal to him. Their friendship continued, probably less because of her apparel than her energy. Often, he waxed ironic about their radically different life styles—hers, from grand royalties for her books, very grand, and his, he would remark, very humble, his royalties enabling him to buy a wheelbarrow in which to trundle his visitors' suitcases up to his house in Rye.

Wharton drove him about like "an avenging angel" in her expensive Panhard, which he designated "a chariot of fire." He enjoyed her confiding in him about her love affair with Morton Fullerton, and admired the passion with which she embraced the affair as well as her writing and her life. Somewhat in hyperbole, he described the "general eagle-power pounced and eagle-flight of her deranging and desolating, raving, burning and destroying energy . . . the Angel of Devastation was the mildest name we knew her by" (Benstock 1994, 197).

For James's seventieth birthday in 1913, Wharton arranged for John Singer Sargent to paint his portrait. She also arranged to have some of her immense royalties diverted to his account, and even raised a subscription to help his finances—arousing his fury when he discovered what she had done. Their last meeting took place in 1914, two years before his death.

Both writers are known today for their novels, and through the films made of them. Yet they were also prolific writers of short fiction published in magazines, in which they drew sharp portraits of social behavior. Some of these stories, including the two in this volume, may be seen as preliminary sketches for later novels.

On February 12, 1891, in the Hotel Westminster in Paris, Henry James wrote in his notebook about the origins of "The Real Thing." His friend, the writer George du Maurier, had been approached by a couple, "An oldish, faded, ruined pair," who had wanted him to find them positions as models for a painter. They had been "all their life stupid and well-dressed, living on a fixed income, at country-houses, watering places and clubs, like so many others of their class in England, and were now utterly unable to *do* anything, had no cleverness, no art nor craft to make use of as a *gagne-pain*—could only show themselves, clumsily for the fine, clean, well-groomed animals that they were, only hope to make a little money by—in this manner—just simply *being*" (James 1947, 102). But, he said, it couldn't be just a story, this "idea." "It must be a picture. It must illustrate something." And for James what it illustrated ultimately was a moral thing, how their "baffled, ineffectual, incompetent" attempt at earning a living this way dramatized an English amateurishness at its worst: how such unprofessional efforts could not hold up against training and genuine qualifications (102, 103). This was to be his focus, and when he got it, he could finally paint his picture.

Interestingly, James's sketch of his idea is already about picture and illustration, as is "The Real Thing." A few years later, a novel, *What Maisie Knew* (1898b), will pick up on the real and the imagined, as will the surpremely ironic and very long novella, "In the Cage" (1898a). But here, in this early story, James gets the idea just right, in all its irony. The notebook entry continues: "Contrast and complication here come from the opposition—to my melancholy Major and his wife—of a couple of little vulgar professional people who *know* . . . " (James 1947, 103).

Hence, for James, *knowing* is more important than appearing, even though appearing just right had seemed to

3

be more real than modeling reality. As for this expression—
knowing—once he had it, he glommed on to it, using it in his
notebook for "The Middle Years" (1893), and then in the
trilogy of his late great novels: *The Wings of the Dove* (1902),
The Golden Bowl (1904), and *The Ambassadors* (1909). Model, picture, illustration: all are part of the Jamesian concern
with the real thing. Thus, the idea which continues to grow
begins here, in a picture that had to be, in all its singleness of
focus, compact. So it is.

In 1922, Edith Wharton published "The Old Maid," a
story based in New York City, where she had grown up,
that represents Old New York in the mid 1800s,[1] when "a
few families ruled, in simplicity and affluence," and where
an illegitimate birth was a subject still so scandalous that the
story was first rejected by several magazines as being too
much for their gentle readers. From the Pavillon Colombe,
in Saint-Brice-sous-Forêt, on June 7, 1921, Wharton wrote
to Bernard Berenson about all the "self-respecting" American magazines who had refused to publish "The Old Maid"
because it dealt with immorality. *The Ladies' Home Journal* had
said, "It's a bit too vigorous for us." *The Metropolitan Magazine*
had found it "powerful but too unpleasant." Wharton asked,
in some astonishment, "Have they never read *The Scarlet Let-
ter* or *Adam Bede*, or my own *Summer*?" (Lewis and Lewis
1988, 443). She, however, was not discouraged; indeed, she
revisited the theme twelve years later in "Roman Fever," a
story which met with great success.

"The Real Thing" (1892) and "The Old Maid" (1922)

4

written thirty years apart, have much in common. Both harbor the germs of later, more famous work. Both are about the "real" and the apparent, revealing, in the juxtaposition, the cruelty involved in the biting accuracy of vision. These stories are about the "real," whatever that might be, and what takes, or seems to take, its place. The judgment of "real" calls into focus views both private and public of the "real" as pictured and as genuine, again, whatever each may be.

After all, "The Real Thing," a story about illustration and painting, is told by an artist. Hence, that famous "center of consciousness," the concept controlling James's tales, is already a center skewed from "reality." The ambiance of the literary thing, as James would have it, and that of the nature of any pictured figures, seen precisely as "natural," might seem at odds, as if artifice and the genuine article were necessarily opposed. But of course, that is exactly the fulcrum on which these two stories turn: the construction of appearance and role-playing, and a reflection on the idea of the "true" thing, concealed through a particular construction.

Each of the four women characters in these stories behaves unpredictably, and one might imagine their actions, decisions, their very ways of existing to be so. How could the world of 2008 resemble the worlds of Wharton in the mid 1800s or James in the late 1890s? Who among us has been trying to pose and has been rejected for a real *poseuse*? Who among us has had a child out of wedlock and has had to suffer the shame of Old New York, when an expectant mother from a "good" family would be sent away to give birth secretly and the child disposed of discretely, perhaps left in a basket to be adopted? Who among us has had to cover up motherhood in so painful a manner? Ultimately the stories return to questions of social truth, "real" truth. One of the crucial sentences in "The Old Maid," reads as cruelly as it does "truthfully." Charlotte, Tina's biological mother, says to Delia, who has been pretending to be Tina's natural (adoptive) mother, "You're her real mother."

At the critical center of the "real" and the stories' connection to the world of the present is the crucial concept of knowing. It is all about knowing. The proper aristocratic wife of James's story, of whom the tweedy and impoverished husband is so proud, is an amateur who does not know how to do anything. She is measured against James's working-class model who knows how to behave as a professional. Wharton measures the smugly privileged and socially accepted wife against the impoverished, unmarried biological mother, whom social custom cannot accept, and who, consequently, cannot avow the truth openly, not even to her own daughter. James's model acts out the illustrative truth—and of course "truth" is the point of both stories, as well as of their devastating social analysis. The cleverer and less "real" of the two women in James's story seems truer to the pictorial representation, a terrible irony. Similarly, one must ask who is the "true" mother in Wharton's story?

In a second reading of these two stories, we might want to ask how the illustration takes over and changes the apparent direction of each. For the apparent "real" should have won out in James's story, and the biological "real" mother should have won out in Wharton's. But neither does. As for the tug of war between the terms, implied and explicit, of "natural," "biological," "actual," "real," and "true"—that is where the interest may lie for the contemporary reader. Once the final choice is made, it finds itself consecrated by the end as if that were to have been, in fact, the only solution. The natural, actual, real solution.

Both Wharton and James hold our attention, unceasingly, by opposing forces, male and female, and, more subtly, by the counterfoils. Take Clem Spender in "The Old Maid," whose child Charlotte bears, to the envy (concealed, even from herself) of Delia, who refused Clem and married wisely and dully. Before her envy is aroused by the color of the thing, the adventure of it all, Delia's society-conscious, tradition-conscious disapproval breaks out: "Was this New York her New York, her safe friendly hypocritical New York, was this James Ralston's house, and this his wife listening to such revelations of dishonor?" Her cousin, guilty of this out-of-wedlock daughter? The hinge, of course, is that Clem loved Delia, as Charlotte stammers out, provoking tears in Delia's eyes. Her peace of mind destroyed, her smugness in her perfect furnishings and perfect husband and perfect life undone, Delia still manages to save it all—the reputations of baby Tina and Charlotte, but at the expense of Charlotte's never being acknowledged as Tina's biological mother.

Still, Delia's struggles of conscience win out at the end, even as Charlotte, the always sacrificing mother, makes another great sacrifice, suggesting that Delia be the last to see Tina before her marriage, though without telling Tina the truth. Delia, in her turn, will insist that "Aunt" Charlotte have the last moment. The story reaches its perfect pitch with this final gesture, just as James does in "The Real Thing," when the artist cold-bloodedly accepts the posed as the truth of art. What a lesson: and, as the artist puts it, although his work has probably suffered from the experience, he is "content to have paid the price—for the memory." But, the reader may want to intervene here, the artist was not actually the one who paid a great price; after all, think of the embarrassment, to put it mildly, of the aristocratic "real" couple. The models were paid for their work, and the gentleman and gentlewoman gain only in melancholy. As we see from his notebooks, James feels little pity for the Englishness of the country-house "amateurs"—as opposed to the cockney model and her Italian friend. So it's the cruel cold truth of art in James's story, and the cruel cold truth of society in Wharton's. Forget nature and the natural, however they are perceived.

The linking of these two writers in the minds of readers scarcely ever has worked in Wharton's favor, as Hermione Lee has pointed out recently in her biography of Wharton. Wharton has often been compared to "The Master," and quite rarely has "The Master" been compared to her (2007).

And yet, we must note that James became the hero of those who formed the American literary canon in the 1940s, while Wharton became the writer whose work has only since the 1970s been coming back into print to receive the acclaim it deserves. And now critics find Wharton's stories and novels always subtle and frequently more complicated (as in the novella chosen here), whereas James seems, especially, of course, in his later work, quite subtle enough right from the start.

That the two authors' reflections on their subjects are preparations for later and better-known works is not without interest, nor indeed that their reflections were both written in France, not in the pragmatic United States or in tradition-steeped England. There is something deeply adventurous about both these works, by two Americans who chose to live abroad, James mostly in England, Wharton mostly in France. The particular kind of objectivity afforded by that distance is worth thinking about: these versions of the real would be developed by both Wharton and James in their subsequent work. Hence, between the "real" of art and the "real" of nature, the second "real" is what goes in parenthesis—not the constructed real, but what would seem to have been given as the truth. In truth, we have, as readers and participants in our own stories, much to learn about the "real."

> Mary Ann Caws
> New York, New York
> November 2007

NOTE

1. "The Old Maid" was originally published in 1922 in *The Red Book Magazine*, and that version, which is out of copyright, is reproduced in this volume. This early version is not without errors, though. While the opening line says, "In the old New York of the 'thirties a few families ruled," later versions, including the one in Wharton's collected tales of Old New York, say, "the old New York of the *'fifties*" (emphasis added, see Wharton 1924). The discrepancy of these dates makes no difference to the context of the tale, which is the desperately strait-laced social situation of the mid 1800s.

WORKS CITED

Benstock, Shari. 1994. *No Gifts from Chance: A Biography of Edith Wharton*. New York: Scribner's.

Caws, Mary Ann. 2006. *Henry James*. New York: Overlook Duckworth.

Edel, Leon. 1978. *Henry James: The Complete Biography* (in 5 vols.). New York: Avon.

James, Henry. 1893. "The Middle Years." *Scribner's Magazine*. New York: Scribner's. May edition.

———. 1898a. "In the Cage." Published in 1936 in *What Maisie Knew; In the Cage; The Pupil*. New York: Scribner's.

———. 1898b. *What Maisie Knew*. London: Heinemann.

———. 1902. *The Wings of the Dove*. New York: Scribner's.

———. 1904. *The Golden Bowl*. New York: Scribner's.

———. 1909. *The Ambassadors*. New York: Scribner's.

———. 1947. *Notebooks of Henry James*. Ed. by F.O. Matthiessen and Kenneth Ballard Murdock. New York: Oxford University Press.

Lee, Hermione. 2007. *Edith Wharton*. New York: Alfred A. Knopf.

Lewis, R.W.B, and Nancy Lewis. 1988. *Letters of Edith Wharton*. New York: Collier Books, Macmillan.

Wharton, Edith. 1924. *Old New York*. New York: D. Appleton Century Inc.

———. 1934. *A Backward Glance*. New York: D. Appleton Century Inc.

Wright, Sarah Bird. 1998. *Edith Wharton A to Z: The Essential Guide to the Life and Work*. New York: Facts on File.

EDITH WHARTON

THE OLD MAID

CHAPTER I

In the old New York of the 'thirties a few families ruled, in simplicity and affluence. Of these were the Ralstons.

The sturdy English and the rubicund and heavier Dutch had mingled to produce a prosperous, prudent, and yet lavish society. To "do things handsomely" had always been a fundamental principle in this cautious world, built up on the fortunes of bankers, India merchants, shipbuilders, and shipchandlers. Those well-fed, slow-moving people, who seemed irritable and dyspeptic to European eyes only because the caprices of the climate had stripped them of superfluous flesh, and strung their nerves a little tighter, lived in a genteel monotony of which the surface was never stirred by the dumb dramas now and then enacted underground. Sensitive souls in those days were like muted keyboards, on which Fate played without a sound.

In this compact society, built of solidly welded blocks, one of the largest areas was filled by the Ralstons and their ramifications. The Ralstons were of middle-class English stock. They had not come to the colonies to die for a creed but to live for a bank-account. The result had been beyond their hopes, and their religion was tinged by their success. An edulcorated Church of England which, under the conciliatory name of the "Episcopal Church of the United States of America," left out the coarser allusions in the Marriage Service, slid over the comminatory passages in the Athanasian Creed, and thought it more respectful to say "Our Father *who*" than "*which*" in the Lord's Prayer, was exactly suited to the spirit of compromise whereon the Ralstons had built themselves up. There was in all the tribe the same instinctive recoil from new religions as from unaccounted-for people. Institutional to the core, they represented the conservative element that holds new societies together as sea-plants bind the seashore.

Compared with the Ralstons, even such traditionalists as the Lovells, the Halseys, or the Vandergraves appeared careless, indifferent to money, almost reckless in their impulses and indecisions. Old John Frederick Ralston, the stout founder of the race, had perceived the difference, and emphasized it to his son, Frederick John, in whom he had scented a faint leaning toward the untried and unprofitable.

"You let the Lannings and the Dagonets and the Spenders take risks and fly kites. It's the county-family blood in 'em: we've nothing to do with that. Look how they're petering out already—the men, I mean. Let your boys marry their girls, if you like (they're wholesome and handsome); though I'd sooner see my grandsons take a Lovell or a Vandergrave, than any of our own kind. But don't let your sons go mooning around with their young fellows, horse-racing, and running down south to those damned springs, and gambling at New Orleans, and all the rest of it. That's how you'll build up the family, and keep the weather out. The way we've always done it."

Frederick John listened, obeyed, married a Halsey, and passively followed in his father's steps. He belonged to the cautious generation of New York gentleman who revered Hamilton and served Jefferson, who longed to lay out New York like Washington, and who laid it out instead like a gridiron, lest they should be thought "undemocratic" by people they secretly looked down upon. Shopkeepers to the marrow, they put in their windows the wares there was most demand for, keeping their private opinions for the back-shop, where through lack of use, they gradually lost substance and color.

The present generation of Ralstons had nothing left in the way of convictions save an acute sense of honor in private and business matters; on the life of the community and the state they took their daily views from the newspapers, and the newspapers they already despised. They themselves had done little to shape the destiny of their country, except to finance the Cause when it had become safe to do so. They were related to many of the great men who had built the Republic; but no Ralston had so far committed himself as to be great. As old John Frederick said, it was safer to be satisfied with three per cent: they regarded heroism as a form of gambling. Yet by merely being so numerous and so similar they had come to have a weight in the community. People said, "The Ralstons," when they wished to invoke a precedent. This attribution of authority had gradually convinced the third generation of its collective importance; and the fourth, to which Delia Ralston's husband belonged, had the ease and simplicity of a ruling class.

Within the limits of their universal caution, the Ralstons fulfilled their obligations as rich and respected citizens. They figured on the boards of all the old-established charities, gave handsomely to thriving institutions, had the best cooks in New York, and when they traveled abroad ordered statuary of the American sculptors in Rome whose reputation was already made. The first Ralston who had brought home a statue had been regarded as a wild fellow; but when it became known that the sculptor had executed several orders for the British aristocracy, it was felt in the family that this too was a three-per-cent investment.

Two marriages with the Dutch Vandergraves had consolidated these qualities of thrift and handsome living, and the carefully built-up Ralston character was now so congenital that Delia Ralston sometimes asked herself whether, were she to turn her own little boy loose in a wilderness, he would not create a small New York there, and be on all its boards of directors.

Delia Lovell had married James Ralston at twenty. The marriage, which had taken place in the month of September, 1840, had been solemnized, as was then the custom, in the drawing-room of the bride's country home, at what is now the corner of Avenue A and Ninety-first Street, overlooking the Sound. Thence her husband had driven her (in Grandmamma Lovell's canary-colored coach with a fringed hammer-cloth), through spreading suburbs and untidy elm-shaded streets, to one of the new houses in Gramercy Park, which the pioneers of the younger set were just beginning to affect; and there, at five-and-twenty, she was established, the mother of two children, the possessor of a generous allowance of pin-money, and, by common consent, one of the handsomest and most popular "young matrons" (as they were called) of her day.

She was thinking placidly and gratefully of these things as she sat one day in her handsome bedroom in Gramercy Park. She was too near to the primitive Ralstons to have as clear a view of them as, for instance, the son in question might one day command: she lived under them as unthinkingly as one lives under the laws of one's country. Yet that tremor in her of the muted keyboard, that secret questioning which sometimes beat in her like wings, would now and then so divide her from them that for a fleeting moment she could survey them in their relation to other things. The moment was always fleeting: she dropped back from it quickly, breathless and a little pale, to her children, her housekeeping, her new dresses, and her kindly Jim.

She thought of him today with a smile of tenderness, remembering how he had told her to spare no expense on her new bonnet. Though she was twenty-five, and twice a mother, her image was still surprisingly fresh. The plumpness then thought seemly in a young matron stretched the gray silk across her bosom, and caused her heavy gold watch-chain—after it left the anchorage of the brooch of St. Peter's in mosaic that fastened her low-cut Cluny collar—to dangle perilously in the void, above a tiny waist buckled into a velvet waist-band. But the shoulders above sloped youthfully under her cashmere scarf, and every movement was as quick as a girl's.

Mrs. Ralston approvingly examined the rosy-cheeked oval set in the blond ruffles of the bonnet on which, in compliance with her husband's instructions, she had spared no expense. It was a cabriolet of white velvet tied with wide satin ribbons and plumed with a crystal-spangled marabou—a wedding bonnet ordered for the marriage of her cousin, Charlotte Lovell, which was to take place that week at St. Mark's-in-the-Bouwerie. Charlotte was making a match exactly like Delia's own: marrying a Ralston, of the Waverly Place branch, than which nothing could be safer, sounder, or more—well, usual. Delia did not know why the word had occurred to her, for it could hardly be postulated, even of the young women of her own narrow clan, that they "usually" married Ralstons; but the soundness, safeness, suitability of the arrangement, did make it typical of the kind of alliance which a nice girl in the nicest set would serenely and blushfully forecast for herself.

Yes—and afterward?

Well—what? And what did this new question mean?

Afterward: why, of course, there was the startled, unpre-
pared surrender to the incomprehensible exigencies of the
young man to whom one had at most accorded a rosy cheek
in return for an engagement ring; there was the large double
bed; the terror of seeing him shaving calmly the next morning, in his shirt-sleeves, through the dressing-room door;
the evasions, insinuations, resigned smiles, and Bible texts
of one's Mamma; the reminder of the phrase "to obey"
in the glittering blur of the Marriage Service; a week or a
month of flushed distress, confusion, embarrassed pleasure;
then the growth of habit, the insidious lulling of the matter-
of-course, dreamless double slumbers in the big white bed,
early-morning discussions and consultations through that
dressing-room door, which had once seemed to open into a
fiery pit scorching the brow of innocence.

And then, the babies; the babies who were supposed to
"make up for everything," and didn't—though they were
such darlings, and one had no definite notion as to what it
was that one had missed, and that they were to make up for.

Yes: Charlotte's fate would be just like hers. Joe Ralston
was so like his second cousin Jim (Delia's James), that Delia
could see no reason why life in the squat brick house in
Waverly Place should not exactly resemble life in the tall
brownstone house in Gramercy Park. Only Charlotte's bedroom would certainly not be as pretty as hers.

She glanced complacently at the French wall-paper that reproduced a watered silk, with a "valanced" border and tassels

between the loops. The mahogany bedstead, covered with a white embroidered counterpane, was symmetrically reflected in the mirror of the wardrobe which matched it. Colored lithographs of the "Four Seasons" by Leopold Robert surmounted groups of family daguerreotypes in deeply recessed gilt frames. The ormolu clock represented a shepherdess sitting on a fallen trunk, a basket of flowers at her feet. A shepherd, stealing up, surprised her with a kiss, while her little dog barked at him from a clump of roses. One knew the profession of the lovers by their crooks and the shape of their hats. This frivolous timepiece had been a wedding-gift from Delia's aunt, Mrs. Manson Mingott, a dashing widow who lived in Paris and was received at the Tuileries. It had been entrusted by her to young Clement Spender, who had come back from Italy for a short holiday just after Delia's marriage; the marriage which might never have been, if Clem Spender could have supported a wife, or had consented to give up painting and Rome for New York and the law. The young man (who looked, already, so odd and foreign and sarcastic) had laughingly assured the bride that her aunt's gift was "the newest thing in the Palais Royal"; and the family, who admired Mrs. Manson Mingott's taste, though they disapproved of her "foreignness," had criticized Delia's putting the clock in her bedroom instead of displaying it on the drawing-room mantel. But she liked, when she woke in the morning, to see the bold shepherd stealing his kiss.

Charlotte would certainly not have such a pretty clock in her bedroom; but then, she had not been used to pretty things. Her father, who had died at thirty of lung-fever, was one of the "poor Lovells." His widow, burdened with a young family, and living all year round "up the River," could not do much for her eldest girl; and Charlotte had entered society in her mother's turned garments, and shod with satin sandals handed down from a defunct great-aunt who had "opened a ball" with General Washington. The old-fashioned Ralston furniture, which Delia already saw herself gradually banishing, would seem sumptuous to Chatty; very likely she would think Delia's gay French timepiece somewhat frivolous, or even "not quite nice." Poor Charlotte had become so serious, so prudish almost, since she had given up balls and taken to visiting the poor! Delia remembered, with ever-recurring wonder, the abrupt change in her: the precise moment at which it had been privately agreed in the family that, after all, Charlotte Lovell was going to be an old maid.

They had not thought so when she came out. Though her mother could not afford to give her more than one new tarlatan dress, and though nearly everything in her appearance was regrettable, from the too bright red of her hair to the too pale brown of her eyes—not to mention the rounds of brick-rose on her cheek-bones, which almost (preposterous thought!) made her look as if she painted— yet these defects were redeemed by a slim waist, a light foot, and a gay laugh; and when her hair was well oiled and brushed for an evening party, so that it looked almost brown, and lay smoothly along her delicate cheeks, under a wreath of red and white camellias, several eligible young men (Joe Ralston among them) were known to have called her pretty.

Then came her illness. She caught cold on a moonlight sleighing-party; the brick-rose circles deepened, and she began to cough. There was a report that she was "going like her father," and she was hurried off to a remote village in Georgia, where she lived alone for a year with an old family governess. When she came back, every one felt at once that there was a change in her. She was pale, and thinner than ever, but with an exquisitely transparent cheek, darker eyes, and redder hair; and the oddness of her appearance was increased by plain dresses of Quakerish cut. She had left off trinkets and watch-chains, always wore the same gray cloak and small close bonnet, and displayed a sudden zeal for visiting the poor. The family explained that during her year in the South she had been shocked by the hopeless degradation of the "poor whites" and their children, and that this revelation of misery had made it impossible for her to return to the light-hearted life of her contemporaries. Everyone agreed, with an exchange of significant glances, that this unnatural state of mind would "pass off in time"; and meanwhile old Mrs. Lovell, Chatty's grandmother, who understood her perhaps better than the others, gave her a little money for her paupers, and lent her a room in the Lovell stables (at the back of the old Mercer Street house) where she gathered about her, in what would afterward have been called a "day-nursery," some of the poor children of the neighborhood.

There was even, among them, the baby girl whose origin had excited such intense curiosity in the neighborhood two or three years earlier, when a veiled lady in handsome clothes had brought it to the hovel of Cyrus Washington, the negro handy-man whose wife Jessamine took in Dr. Lanskell's washing. Dr. Lanskell was the chief practitioner of the day, and presumably versed in the secret history of every household from the Battery to Union Square; but though beset by inquisitive patients, he had invariably declared himself unable to identify Jessamine's "veiled lady," or to hazard a guess as to the origin of the hundred-dollar bill pinned to the baby's cloak.

The hundred dollars were never renewed; the lady never reappeared; but the baby lived healthily and happily with Jessamine's pickaninnies, and as soon as it could toddle, was brought to Chatty Lovell's day-nursery, where it appeared (like its fellow paupers) in little garments cut down from her old dresses, and socks knitted by her untiring hands. Delia, absorbed in her own babies, had nevertheless dropped in once or twice at the nursery, and had come away wishing that Chatty's maternal instinct might find its normal outlet in marriage and motherhood. The married cousin confusedly felt that her own affection for her handsome children was a mild and measured sentiment compared with Chatty's fierce passion for the plebeian waifs in Grandmamma Lovell's stable.

And then, to the general surprise, Charlotte Lovell engaged herself to Joe Ralston. It was known that Joe had "admired her" the year she came out. She was a graceful dancer, and Joe, who was tall and nimble, had footed it with her through many a reel and Schottisch. By the end of the winter all the match-makers were predicting that something would come of it; but when Delia playfully sounded her cousin, the girl's evasive answer and burning brow seemed to imply that her suitor had changed his mind, and no more questions had been asked. Now it became evident that there had, in fact, been an old romance, probably followed by that exciting incident, a "misunderstanding;" but at last all was well, and the bells of St. Mark's were about to ring in happier days for Charlotte. "Ah, when she has her first baby," the Ralston mothers chorused.

"Chatty!" Delia exclaimed, pushing back her chair as she saw her cousin's image reflected in the glass over her shoulder.

Charlotte Lovell had paused in the doorway. "They told me you were here—so I ran up."

"Of course, darling. How handsome you do look in your poplin! I always said you needed rich materials. I'm so thankful to see you out of brown cashmere." Delia lifted her hands, and raising the white bonnet from her dark polished head, shook it so that the crystals glittered.

"I hope you like it? It's for your wedding," she laughed.

Charlotte Lovell stood motionless. In her mother's old dove-colored poplin, freshly banded with rows of crimson velvet ribbon, an ermine tippet crossed on her bosom, and a new beaver bonnet with a falling feather, she had already something of the assurance and majesty of a married woman.

"And you know your hair *is* darker, darling," Delia added, still hopefully surveying her.

"Darker? It's gray," Charlotte broke out in her deep voice, pushing back one of the pomaded bands that framed her face, and showing a white lock on her temple. "You needn't save up your bonnet; I'm not going to be married," she added harshly, with a smile that showed her teeth in a fleeting glare.

Delia had just enough presence of mind to lay down the white bonnet, marabou up, before she flung herself on her cousin.

"Not going to be married? Charlotte, are you perfectly crazy?"

"Why is it crazy to do what I think right?"

"But people said you were going to marry him the year you came out. And no one understood what happened then. And now—how can it possibly be right? You simply *can't!*" Delia incoherently summed up.

"Oh—people!" said Charlotte wearily.

Her married cousin looked at her with a start. Something thrilled in her voice that Delia had never heard in it, or in any other human voice, before. Its echo seemed to set their familiar world rocking, and the Axminster carpet actually heaved under Delia's shrinking slippers.

—

Charlotte stood staring ahead of her with strained lids. In the pale brown of her eyes Delia noticed the green specks that floated there when she was angry or excited.

"Charlotte—where on earth have you come from?" she cried, drawing the girl down to the sofa.

"Come from?"

"Yes. You look as if you'd seen a ghost—an army of ghosts."

The same snarling smile drew up Charlotte's lip. "I've seen Joe," she said.

"Well? . . . Oh, Chatty," Delia cried, abruptly illuminated, "you don't mean to say that you're going to let any little thing in Joe's past—not that I've ever heard the least hint, never. But if there were—" She drew a deep breath, and bravely proceeded to extremities. "Even if you've heard that he's been—that he's had a child—of course he would have provided for it before—"

The girl shook her head. "I know; you needn't go on. 'Men will be men'; but it's not that."

"Tell me what it is."

Charlotte Lovell looked about the sunny, prosperous room as if it were the image of her world, and that world were a prison she must break out of. She lowered her head. "I want—to get away," she panted.

"Get away? From Joe?"

"From his ideas—the Ralston ideas."

Delia bridled—after all, she was a Ralston! "The Ralston

ideas? I haven't found them—so unbearably unpleasant to live with," she smiled a little tartly.

"No. But it was different with you: they didn't ask you to give up things."

"What things?" What in the world, Delia wondered, had poor Charlotte, that anyone could want her to give up? She had always been in the position of taking rather than of having to surrender. "Can't you explain to me, dear?" Delia urged.

"My poor children—he says I'm to give them up," cried the girl in a stricken whisper.

"Give them up? Give up helping them?"

"Seeing them—looking after them. Give them up altogether. He got his mother to explain to me. After—after we have children, he's afraid—afraid our children might catch things. . . . He'll give me money, of course, to pay some one—a hired person to look after them. He thought that handsome," Charlotte broke out in a sob. She flung off her bonnet and smothered her weeping in the cushions.

Delia sat perplexed. Of all unforeseen complications this was surely the least imaginable. And with all the acquired Ralston that was in her she could not help seeing the force of Joe's objection, could almost find herself agreeing with him. No one in New York had forgotten the death of the poor Henry van der Luydens's only child, from smallpox caught at the circus to which an unprincipled nurse had surreptitiously taken him. After that warning, parents felt justified in every precaution against contagion. And poor people were so ignorant and careless, and their children, of course, so perpetually exposed to everything catching. No, Joe Ralston was certainly right, and Charlotte almost insanely unreasonable. But it would be useless to tell her so now. Instinctively, Delia temporized.

"After all," she whispered to the prone ear, "if it's only after you have children—you may not have any—for some time."

"Oh, yes, I shall!" came back in anguish from the cushions.

Delia smiled with matronly superiority. "Really, Chatty, I don't quite see how you can know. You don't understand."

Charlotte Lovell lifted herself up. Her collar of Brussels lace hung in a crumpled wisp on the loose folds of her bodice, and through the disorder of her hair the white lock glimmered haggardly. In the pale brown of her eyes the little green specks floated like leaves in a trout-pool.

"Poor girl," Delia thought, "how old and ugly she looks! More than ever like an old maid; and she seems to have no idea that she'll never have another chance."

"You must try to be sensible, Chatty dear. After all, one's own babies have the first claim."

"That's just it." The girl seized her fiercely by the wrists. "How can I give up my own baby?"

"Your—your?" Delia's world again began to waver under her. "Which of the poor little waifs, dearest, do you call your own baby?" she questioned patiently.

Charlotte looked her straight in the eyes. "I call my own baby my own baby."

"Your own—? You're hurting my wrists, Chatty." Delia freed herself, forcing a smile. "Your own—?"

"My own little girl, the one that Jessamine and Cyrus—"

"Oh—" Delia Ralston gasped.

The two cousins sat silent, facing each other; but Delia looked away. It came over her with a shudder of repugnance that such things should not have been spoken in her bedroom, so near the spotless nursery across the passage. Mechanically she smoothed the folds of her silk skirt, which her cousin's embrace had crumpled. Then she looked again at Charlotte's eyes, and her own melted.

"Oh, poor Chatty—poor Chatty!" She held out her arms to her cousin.

CHAPTER II

The shepherd continued to steal his kiss from the shepherdess, and the clock in the fallen trunk continued to tick out the minutes.

Delia, petrified, sat unconscious of their passing, her cousin clasped to her. She was dumb with the horror and amazement of learning that her own blood ran in the veins of the anonymous foundling, the "hundred-dollar baby" about whom New York had so long furtively jested and conjectured. It was her first contact with the nether side of the smooth social surface, and she sickened at the thought that such things were, and that she, Delia Ralston, should be hearing of them in her own house, from the lips of the victim! For Chatty of course was a victim—but whose? She had spoken no name, and Delia could put no question: the horror of it sealed her lips. Her mind had instantly raced back over Chatty's past; but she saw no masculine figure in it but Joe Ralston's. And to connect Joe with the episode was obviously unthinkable. Some one in the South, then? But no: Charlotte had been ill when she left—and in a flash Delia understood the real nature of that illness, and of the girl's disappearance. But from such speculations too, her mind recoiled, and instinctively she fastened on something she could still grasp: Joe Ralston's attitude about Chatty's paupers. Of course Joe could not let his wife risk bringing home contagion—that was safe ground to dwell on. Her own Jim would have felt in the same way; and she would certainly have agreed with him.

Her eyes traveled back to the clock. She always thought of Clem Spender when she looked at the clock, and suddenly she wondered—if things had been different—what *he* would have said if she had made such an appeal to him as Charlotte had made to Joe. The thing seemed inconceivable; yet in a flash of mental readjustment she saw herself as his wife, she saw her children as his; she pictured herself asking him to let her go on caring for the poor waifs in the Mercer Street stable, and she distinctly heard his laugh and his light answer: "Why on earth did you ask, you little goose? Do you take me for such a Pharisee as that?"

Yes, that was Clem Spender all over—tolerant, reckless,

indifferent to consequences, always doing the kind thing at the moment, and too often leaving others to pay the score. "There's something cheap about Clem," Jim had once said in his heavy way. Delia Ralston roused herself and pressed her cousin closer. "Chatty, tell me," she whispered.

"There's nothing more."

"I mean, about yourself—this thing—this—" Clem Spender's voice was still in her ears. "You loved some one," she breathed.

"Yes. That's over. . . . Now it's only the child. . . . And I could love Joe—in another way." Chatty Lovell straightened herself, wan and frowning.

"I need the money—I must have it for my baby, or else they'll send it to an institution." She paused. "But that's not all. I want to marry—to be a wife, like all of you. I should have loved Joe's children—our children. Life doesn't stop."

"No: I suppose not. But you speak as if—as if—the person who took advantage of you—"

"No one took advantage of me. I was lonely and unhappy. I met someone who was lonely and unhappy. People don't all have your luck. We were both too poor to marry each other—and Mother would never have consented. And so one day—one day before he said good-by—"

"He said good-by?"

"Yes. He was going to leave the country."

"To leave the country—knowing?"

"How was he to know? He doesn't live here. He'd just come back—come back to see his family—for a few weeks—" She broke off, her thin lips pressed together upon her secret.

There was a silence. Delia stared at the bold shepherd.

"Come back from where?" she suddenly asked in a low tone.

"Oh, what does it matter? You wouldn't understand," Charlotte broke off irritably, in the very words her married cousin had compassionately addressed to her virginity.

A slow blush rose to Delia's cheek: she felt oddly humiliated by the rebuke conveyed in that contemptuous retort. She seemed to herself shy, ineffectual, as incapable as an ignorant girl of dealing with the abominations that Charlotte was thrusting on her. But suddenly some fierce feminine intuition struggled and woke in her. She forced her eyes upon her cousin's.

"You won't tell me who it was?"

"What's the use? I haven't told anybody."

"Then why have you come to me?"

Charlotte's stony face broke up in weeping. "It's for my baby—my baby—"

Delia did not heed her. "How can I help you if I don't know?" she insisted in a harsh, dry voice: her heartbeats were so violent that they felt like a throttling hand at her throat.

Charlotte made no answer.

"Come back from where?" Delia doggedly repeated; and at that, with a long wail, the girl flung her hands up, screening her eyes. "He always thought you'd wait for him," she sobbed out, "and then, when he found you hadn't—and that you were marrying Jim—he heard it just as he was sailing. . . . He didn't know it till Mrs. Mingott asked him to bring the clock for your wedding—"

"Stop—stop," Delia cried, springing to her feet. She had provoked the avowal, and now that it had come, she felt that it had been gratuitously and indecently thrust upon her. Was this New York, *her* New York, her safe, friendly, hypocritical New York, was this James Ralston's house, and this his wife listening to such revelations of dishonor?

Charlotte stood up in her turn. "I knew it—I knew it! You think worse of my baby now, instead of better. . . . Oh, why did you make me tell you? I knew you'd never understand. I'd always cared for him, ever since I came out; that was why I wouldn't marry any one else. But I knew there was no hope for me—he never looked at anybody but you. And then, when he came back four years ago, and there was no *you* for him any more, he began to notice me, to be kind, to talk to me about his life and his painting—" She drew a deep breath, and her voice cleared. "That's over—all over. It's as if I couldn't either hate him or love him. There's only the child now—my child. He doesn't even know of it—why should he? It's none of his business; it's nobody's business but mine. But surely you must see that I can't give up my baby."

Delia Ralston stood speechless, looking away from her cousin in a growing horror. She had lost all sense of reality, all feeling of safety and self-reliance. Her impulse was to close her ears to the other's appeal as a child buries its head from midnight terrors. At last she drew herself up, and spoke with dry lips.

"But what do you mean to do? Why have you come to me? Why have you told me all this?"

"Because he loved you!" Charlotte Lovell stammered out; and the two women stood and faced each other.

Slowly the tears rose to Delia's eyes and rolled down her cheeks, moistening her parched lips. Through them she saw her cousin's haggard countenance waver and droop like a drowning face under water. Things half guessed, obscurely felt, surged up from unsuspected depths in her. It was almost as if, for a moment, this other woman were telling her of her own secret past, putting into crude words all the trembling silences of her heart.

The worst of it was, as Charlotte said, that they must act now; there was not a day to lose. Chatty was right—it was impossible that she should marry Joe if to do so meant giving up the child. But, in any case, how could she marry him without telling him the truth? And was it conceivable that, after hearing it, he should not repudiate her? All these questions spun agonizingly through Delia's brain, and through them glimmered the persistent vision of the child—Clem Spender's child—growing up on charity, in a negro hovel, or herded in one of the plague-houses they called asylums. No: the child came first—she felt it in every fiber of her body. But what should she do, of whom take counsel, how advise the wretched creature who had come to her in Clement's name? Delia glanced about her desperately, and then turned back to her cousin.

"You must give me time. I must think. You ought not to marry him—and yet all the arrangements are made; and the wedding presents. . . . There would be a scandal. . . . It would kill Granny Lovell."

Charlotte answered in a low voice: "There *is* no time. I must decide now."

Delia pressed her hands against her breast. "I tell you I must think. I wish you would go home—or, no: stay here—your mother mustn't see your eyes. Jim's not coming home till late; you can wait in this room till I come back." She had opened the wardrobe, and was reaching up for a plain bonnet and heavy veil.

"Stay here? But where are you going?"

"I don't know. I want to walk—to get the air. I think I want to be alone." Feverishly she had unfolded her Paisley shawl, tied on bonnet and veil, thrust her mittened hands into her muff. Charlotte, without moving, stared at her dumbly from the sofa.

"You'll wait?" Delia insisted, on the threshold.

"Yes; I'll wait."

Delia shut the door and hurried down the stairs.

CHAPTER III

She had spoken the truth in saying that she did not know where she was going. She simply wanted to get away from

Charlotte's unbearable face, and from the immediate atmosphere of her tragedy. Outside, in the open, perhaps it would be easier to think.

As she skirted the park-rails, she saw her rosy children playing, under their nurse's eye, with the pampered progeny of other Park-dwellers. The little girl had on her new plaid velvet bonnet and white tippet, and the boy his Highland cap and broadcloth spencer. How happy and jolly they looked! The nurse spied her, but she shook her head, waved at the group, and hurried on.

She walked and walked through the familiar streets decked with bright winter sunshine. It was early afternoon, an hour when the gentlemen had just returned to their offices, and there were few pedestrians in Irving Place and Union Square. Delia crossed the Square to Broadway.

The Lovell house in Mercer Street was a sturdy, old-fashioned brick dwelling. A large stable adjoined it, opening on an alley such as Delia, on her honeymoon trip to England, had heard called a "mews." She turned into the alley, entered the stable court, and pushed open a door. In a shabby whitewashed room a dozen children, gathered about a stove, were playing with broken toys. The Irishwoman who had charge of them was cutting out small garments on a broken-legged deal table. She raised a friendly face, recognizing Delia as the lady who had once or twice been to see the children with Miss Charlotte.

Delia paused, embarrassed.

"I—I came to ask if you need any new toys," she stammered.

"That we do, ma'am. And many another thing too, though Miss Charlotte tells me I'm not to beg of the ladies that comes to see our poor darlin's."

"Oh, you may beg of me, Bridget," Mrs. Ralston answered, smiling. "Let me see your babies—it's so long since I've been here."

The children had stopped playing, and huddled against their nurse, gazed up open-mouthed at the rich, rustling lady. One little girl with pale brown eyes and scarlet cheeks was dressed in a plaid alpaca frock trimmed with imitation coral buttons that Delia remembered. They had been on Charlotte's "best dress" the year she came out. Delia stooped and took up the child. Its curly hair was brown, the exact color of the eyes—thank heaven! But the eyes had the same little green spangles floating in their transparency. Delia sat down, and the little girl, standing on her knee, gravely fingered her watch-chain.

"Oh, ma'am—maybe her shoes'll soil your skirt. The floor ain't none too clean."

Delia shook her head, and pressed the child against her. She had forgotten the other gazing babies and their wardress. The little creature on her knee was made of different stuff—it had not needed the plaid alpaca and coral buttons to single her out. Her brown curls grew in points on her high forehead, exactly as Clement Spender's did. Delia laid a burning cheek against the forehead.

"Baby want my lovely yellow chain?"

Baby did.

Delia unfastened it and hung it about the child's neck. The other babies clapped and crowed, but the little girl, gravely dimpling, continued to finger the chain in silence.

"Oh, ma'am, you can't leave that fine chain on little Teeny. When she has to go back to those blacks—"

"What is her name?"

"Teena they call her, I believe. It don't seem a Christian name, har'ly."

Delia was silent.

"What I say is, her cheeks is too red. And she coughs too easy. Always one cold and another. Here, Teeny, leave the lady go."

Delia stood up, loosening the tender arms.

"She doesn't want to leave go of you, ma'am. Miss Chatty ain't been in yet, and she's kinder lonesome without her. She don't play like the other children, somehow. . . . Teeny, you look at that lovely chain you've got. . . . There, there now!"

"Good-by, Clementina," Delia whispered below her breath. She kissed the pale brown eyes, the curly crown, and dropped her veil on rushing tears. In the stableyard she dried them on her large embroidered handkerchief, and stood hesitating. Then with a decided step she turned toward home.

The house was as she had left it, except that the children had come in; she heard them romping in the nursery as she went down the passage to her bedroom. Charlotte Lovell was seated on the sofa, upright and rigid, as Delia had left her.

"Chatty—Chatty, I've thought it out. Listen: Whatever happens, the baby sha'n't stay with those people. I mean to keep her."

Charlotte stood up, tall and white. The eyes in her thin face had grown so dark that they seemed like spectral hollows in a skull. She opened her lips to speak, and then, snatching at her handkerchief, pressed it to her mouth, and sank down again. A red trickle dripped through the handkerchief onto her poplin skirt.

"Charlotte—Charlotte!" Delia screamed, on her knees beside her cousin. Charlotte's head slid back against the cushions, and the trickle ceased. She closed her eyes, and Delia, seizing a vinaigrette from the dressing-table, held it to her pinched nostrils. The room was filled with an acrid aromatic scent.

Charlotte's lids lifted. "Don't be frightened. I still spit blood sometimes—not often. My lung is nearly healed. But it's the terror—"

"No, no: there's to be no more terror. I tell you I've thought it all out. Jim is going to let me take the baby."

The girl raised herself haggardly. "Jim? Have you told him? Is that where you've been?"

"No, darling. I've only been to see the baby."

"Oh!" Charlotte moaned, leaning back again. Delia took her own handkerchief, and wiped away the tears that were raining down her cousin's cheeks.

"You mustn't cry, Chatty; you must be brave. Your little girl and his—how could you think? But you must give me time: I must manage it in my own way. . . . Only trust me."

Charlotte's lips stirred faintly.

"The tears—don't dry them, Delia. I like to feel them."

The two cousins leaned against each other without speaking. The ormolu clock ticked out the measure of their mute communion in minutes, quarters, a half-hour, then an hour: the day declined and darkened; the shadows lengthened across the garlands of the Axminster carpet and the broad white bed. There was a knock.

"The children's waiting to say their grace before supper, ma'am."

"Yes, Eliza. Let them say it to you. I'll come later." As the nurse's steps receded, Charlotte Lovell disengaged herself from Delia's embrace.

"Now I can go," she said.

"You're not too weak, dear? I can send for a coach to take you home."

"No, no; it would frighten Mother. And I shall like walking now, in the darkness. Sometimes the world used to seem all one awful glare to me. There were days when I thought the sun would never set. And then there was the moon at night." She laid her hands on her cousin's shoulders. "Now it's different. By and by I sha'n't hate the light."

The two women kissed each other, and Delia whispered: "Tomorrow."

CHAPTER IV

The Ralstons gave up old customs reluctantly, but once they had adopted a new one, they found it impossible to understand why everyone else did not do likewise.

When Delia, who came of the laxer Lovells, and was naturally inclined to novelty, had first proposed to her husband to dine at six o' clock instead of two, his malleable young face had become as relentless as that of the old original Ralston in his grim colonial portrait. But after a two days' resistance, he had come round to his wife's view, and now smiled contemptuously at the obstinacy of those who clung to a heavy midday meal and high tea.

"There's nothing I hate like narrow-mindedness. Let people eat when they like, for all I care: it's their narrow-mindedness that I can't stand."

Delia was thinking of this as she sat in the drawing-room (her mother would have called it the parlor) waiting for her husband's return. She had just had time to smooth her glossy braids, and slip on the black-and-white striped silk with cherry pipings which was his favorite dress. The drawing-room, with its Nottingham lace curtains looped back under florid gilt cornices, its marble center-table on a carved rosewood foot, and its old-fashioned mahogany armchairs covered with one of the new French silk damasks in a tart shade of apple-green, was one for any young wife to be proud of. The rosewood whatnots on each side of the folding doors that led into the dining-room were adorned with tropical shells, feldspar vases, an alabaster model of the Leaning Tower of Pisa, a pair of obelisks made of scraps of porphyry and serpentine picked up by the young couple in the Roman Forum, a small bust of Clytie in *biscuit de Sèvres*, and four old-fashioned figures of the Seasons in Chelsea ware, that had to be left among the newer knick-knacks because they had belonged to Great-grand-mamma Ralston. On the damask wall-paper hung large dark steel-engravings of Cole's "Voyage of Life," and on the table lay handsomely tooled copies of Turner's "Rivers of France," Drake's "Culprit Fay," Crabbe's "Tales," and "The Book of Beauty," containing portraits of the British peeresses who had participated in the Earl of Eglinton's tournament.

As Delia sat there, before the hard-coal fire in its arched opening of black marble, her citron-wood work-table at her side, and one of the new French lamps shedding a pleasant light on the center-table from under a crystal-fringed shade, she asked herself how she could have passed, in such a short time, so completely out of her usual circle of impressions and convictions—so much farther than ever before beyond the Ralston horizon. Here it was, closing in on her again, as if the very plaster ornaments of the ceiling, the forms of the furniture, the cut of her dress, had been built out of Ralston prejudices, and turned to adamant by the touch of Ralston hands.

She must have been mad, she thought, to have committed herself so far to Charlotte; yet turn about as she would in the ever-tightening circle of the problem, she could still discover no other issue. Somehow, it lay with her to save Clem Spender's baby.

She heard the sound of the latchkey (her heart had never beat so high at it), and the putting down of a tall hat on the hall console—or two tall hats, was it? The drawing-room door opened, and two high-stocked and ample-coated young men came in—two Jim Ralstons, so to speak. Delia had never before noticed how much her husband and his cousin Joe were alike: it made her feel how justified she was in always thinking of the Ralstons collectively.

She would not have been young, and tender, and a happy wife, if she had not thought Joe but an indifferent copy of her Jim; yet, allowing for defects in the reproduction, there remained a striking likeness between the two tall, athletic figures, the short, sanguine faces with straight noses, straight whiskers, straight brows, the candid blue eyes and sweet, selfish smiles. Only, at the present moment, Joe looked like Jim with a toothache.

"Look here, my dear: here's a young man who's asked to take potluck with us," Jim smiled, with the confidence of a well-nourished husband who knows that he can always bring a friend home unannounced.

"How nice of you, Joe! Do you suppose he can put up with oyster soup and a stuffed goose?" Delia beamed upon her husband.

"I knew it! I told you so, my dear chap! He said you wouldn't like it—that you'd be fussed about the dinner. Wait till you're married, Joseph Ralston!" Jim brought down a genial paw on his cousin's bottle-green shoulder, and Joe grimaced as if the tooth had stabbed him.

"It's excessively kind of you, Cousin Delia, to take me in this evening. The fact is—"

"Dinner first, my boy, if you don't mind! A bottle of Burgundy will brush away the blue devils. Your arm to your cousin, please; I'll just go and see that the wine is brought up."

Oyster soup, broiled shad, stuffed goose, corn fritters, and green peppers, followed by one of Grandmamma Ralston's famous caramel custards: through all her mental anguish, Delia was faintly aware of a secret pride in her achievement. Certainly it would serve to confirm the rumor that Jim Ralston could always bring a friend home to dine without notice. The Ralston and Lovell wines rounded off the effect, and even Joe's drawn face had mellowed by the time the Lovell Madeira started westward. Delia marked the change when the two young men rejoined her in the drawing-room.

"And now, my dear fellow, you'd better tell her the whole story," Jim counseled, pushing an armchair toward his cousin.

The young woman, bent above her wool-work, listened with lowered lids and flushed cheeks. As a married woman —as a mother—Joe hoped she would think him justified in speaking to her frankly: he had her husband's authority to do so.

"Oh, go ahead, go ahead," chafed the exuberant after-dinner Jim from the hearth-rug.

Delia listened, considered, let the bridegroom flounder on through his exposition. Her needle hung like a sword of Damocles above the canvas: she saw at once that Joe depended on her trying to win Charlotte over to his way of thinking. But he was very much in love: at a word from Delia, she understood that he would yield, and Charlotte gain her point, save the child, and marry him.

How easy it was, after all! A friendly welcome, a good dinner, a ripe wine, and the memory of Charlotte's eyes—so much the more expressive for all that they had looked upon. A secret envy stabbed the wife who had lacked this last enlightenment.

How easy it was—and yet it must not be! Whatever happened, she could not let Charlotte Lovell marry Joe Ralston. All the traditions of honor and probity in which she had been brought up forbade her to connive at such a plan. She could conceive—had already conceived—of high-handed measures, swift and adroit defiances of precedent, subtle revolts against the heartlessness of social routine. But a lie she could never connive at. The idea of Charlotte's marrying Joe Ralston—her own Jim's cousin—without revealing her past to him, seemed to Delia as dishonorable as it would have seemed to any Ralston. And to tell him the truth would at once put an end to the marriage; of that even Chatty was aware. Social tolerance was not dealt in the same measure to men and to women, and neither Delia nor Charlotte had ever wondered why: like all the young women of their class they simply bowed to the ineluctable.

No: there was no escape from the dilemma. As clearly as it was Delia's duty to save Clem Spender's child, so clearly, also, she seemed destined to sacrifice his mistress. As the thought pressed on her, she remembered Charlotte's wistful cry: "I want to be married, like all of you," and her heart tightened. But yet it must not be.

"I make every allowance," Joe was droning on, "for my sweet girl's ignorance and inexperience—for her lovely purity. How could a man wish his future wife to be—to be otherwise? You're with me, Jim? And Delia? I've told her, you understand, that she shall always have a special sum for her poor children, in addition to her pin-money—on that she may absolutely count. God! I'm willing to draw up a deed, a settlement, before a lawyer, if she says so. I admire, I appreciate her generosity. But I ask you, Delia, as a mother— mind you, now, I want your frank opinion. If you think I can stretch a point—can let her go on giving her personal care to the children until—until"—a flush of pride suffused the po-tential father's brow—"till nearer duties claim her. . . . Why, I'm more than ready—if you'll tell her so. I undertake," Joe proclaimed, suddenly tingling with the memory of his last glass, "to make it right with my mother, whose prejudices, of course, while I respect them, I can never allow to—to come between me and my own convictions." He sprang to his feet, and beamed on his dauntless double in the chimney-mirror. "My convictions," he flung back at it.

"Hear, hear!" cried Jim emotionally.

Delia's needle gave the canvas a sharp prick, and she pushed her work aside.

"I think I understand you both, Joe. Certainly, in Charlotte's place, I should never give up those children."

"There you are, my dear fellow!" Jim triumphed, as proud of this vicarious courage as of the perfection of the dinner.

"Never," said Delia. "Especially, I mean, the foundlings—there are two, I think. Those children always die if they are sent to asylums. That is what is haunting Chatty."

"Poor innocents! How I love her for loving them! That there should be such scoundrels upon this earth unpunished! Delia, will you tell her that I'll do whatever—"

"Gently, old man, gently," Jim admonished him, with a flash of Ralston caution.

"Well, whatever—in reason—"

Delia lifted an arresting hand. "I'll tell her, Joe: she will be grateful. But it's of no use."

"No use? What more—?"

"Nothing more—except this. Charlotte has had a return of her old illness. She coughed blood here today. You must not marry her."

There: it was done. She stood up, trembling in every bone, and feeling herself pale to the lips. Had she done right? Had she done wrong? And would she ever know?

Poor Joe turned on her a face as wan as hers: he clutched the back of his armchair, his head drooping forward like an old man's. His lips moved, but made no sound.

"My God!" Jim stammered. "But you know you've got to pull yourself together, old boy."

"I'm—I'm so sorry for you, Joe. She'll tell you tomorrow," Delia faltered, while her husband continued to proffer heavy consolations.

"Take it like a man, old chap. Think of yourself—your future. Can't be, you know. Delia's right; she always *is*. Better get it over—better face the music now than later."

"Now than later," Joe echoed with a tortured grin; and it occurred to Delia that never before in the course of his easy, good-natured life had he had—any more than her Jim—to give up anything his heart was set on. Even the vocabulary of renunciation, and its conventional gestures, were unfamiliar to him.

"But I don't understand. I can't give her up," he declared, blinking away boyish tears.

"Think of the children, my dear fellow; it's your duty," Jim admonished him, checking a glance of pride at Delia's wholesome comeliness.

In the long conversation that followed between the cousins—argument, counter-argument, sage counsel, and hopeless protest—Delia took but an occasional part. She knew well enough what the end would be. The bridegroom who had feared that his bride might bring home contagion from her visits to the poor would not knowingly implant disease in his race. Nor was that all. Too many sad instances of mothers prematurely fading, and leaving their husbands alone with a young flock to rear, must be pressing upon

Joe's memory. Ralstons, Lovells, Lannings, Archers, van der Luydens—which one of them had not some grave to care for in a distant cemetery, graves of young relatives "in a decline," sent abroad to be cured by balmy Italy? The Protestant graveyards of Rome and Pisa were full of New York names; and the vision of that familiar pilgrimage with a dying wife was one to turn the most ardent Ralston cold. And all the while, as she listened with bent head, Delia kept repeating to herself: "This is easy; but how am I to tell Charlotte?"

When poor Joe, late that evening, wrung her hand with a stammered farewell, she called him back abruptly.

"You must let me see her first, please; you must wait till she sends for you." And she winced a little at the alacrity of his acceptance. But no amount of rhetorical bolstering-up could make it easy for a young man to face what lay ahead of Joe; and her final glance at him was one of compassion.

The front door closed upon Joe, and she was roused by her husband's touch on her shoulder.

"I never admired you more, darling. My wise Delia!"

Her head bent back, she took his kiss, and then drew away. The sparkle in his eyes she understood to be as much an invitation to her bloom as a tribute to her sagacity.

"What should you have done, Jim, if I'd had to tell you about myself what I've just told Joe about Chatty?"

A slight frown showed that he thought the question negligible, and hardly in her usual taste. "Come!" His strong arm entreated her.

She continued to stand away from him, with grave eyes. "Poor Chatty! Nothing left now—"

His own eyes grew grave in sympathy. At such moments he was still the sentimental boy whom she could manage.

"Ah, poor Chatty, indeed!" He groped for the readiest panacea. "Lucky, after all, she has those paupers, isn't it? I suppose a woman *must* have children to love—somebody else's if not her own." It was evident that the remedy had already relieved his pain.

"Yes," she agreed, "I see no other comfort for her. I'm sure Joe will feel that too. Between us, darling,"—and now she let him have her hands—"between us, you and I must see to it that she keeps her babies."

"Her babies?" He smiled at the possessive pronoun. "Of course, poor girl! Unless she's sent to Italy?"

"Oh, she won't be that—where's the money to come from? And, besides, she'd never leave Aunt Lovell. But I thought, dear, if I might tell her tomorrow—you see, I'm not exactly looking forward to my talk with her—if I might tell her that you would let me look after the baby she's most worried about, the poor little foundling girl who has no name and no home—if I might put aside a fixed sum from my pin-money—"

Their hands glowed together; she lifted her flushing face to his. Manly tears were in his eyes: ah, how he triumphed in her health, her wisdom, her generosity!

"Not a penny from your pin-money!"

She feigned discouragement and wonder. "Think,

dear—if I'd had to give you up!"

"Not a penny from your pin-money, I say—but as much more as you need, to help poor Chatty's pauper. There—will that content you?"

"Dearest! When I think of our own upstairs!" They held each other, awed by that evocation.

CHAPTER V

Charlotte Lovell, at the sound of her cousin's step on the threshold, lifted a fevered face from the pillow.

The bedroom, dim and close, smelt of eau de Cologne and fresh linen. Delia, blinking in from the bright winter sun, had to feel her way through a twilight obstructed by dark mahogany.

"I want to see your face, Chatty—unless your head aches too much?"

Charlotte sighed, "No," and Delia drew back the heavy window-curtains and let a ray of light into the room. In it, she saw the girl's head livid against the bed-linen, the brick-red circles again visible under darkly shadowed lids. Just so poor Cousin So-and-so had looked, the week before she sailed for Italy!

"Delia!" Charlotte breathed.

Delia approached the bed, and stood looking down at her cousin with new eyes. Yes: it had been easy enough, the night before, to dispose of Chatty's future as if it were her own—but now?

"Darling—"

"Oh, begin, please," the girl interrupted, "or I shall know that what's coming is too dreadful!"

"Chatty, dearest, if I promised you too much—"

"Jim won't let you take my child? I knew it! Shall I always go on dreaming things that can never be?"

Delia, her tears running down, knelt by the bed and gave her fresh hand into the other's burning clutch.

"Don't think that, dear; think only of what you'd like best."

"Like best?" The girl rose sharply against her pillows, alive to the hot fingertips.

"You can't marry Joe, dear—can you—and keep little Tina?" Delia continued.

"Not keep her with me, no—but somewhere where I could slip off to see her. Oh, I had hoped such follies!"

"Give up follies, Charlotte. Keep her where? See your own child in secret? Always in dread of disgrace? Of wrong to your other children? Have you ever thought of that?"

"Oh, my poor head won't think! You're trying to tell me that I must give her up?"

"No, dear—but that you must not marry Joe."

Charlotte sank back on the pillow, her eyes half-closed. "I tell you I must make my child a home. Delia, you're too blessed to understand!"

"Think of yourself blessed too, Chatty. You sha'n't give up your baby. She shall live with you: you shall take care of her—for me."

"For you?"

"I promised you I'd take her, didn't I? But not that you should marry Joe. Only that I would make a home for your baby. Well, that's done: you shall always be together."

Charlotte clung to her and sobbed. "But Joe—I can't tell him, I can't." She put back Delia suddenly. "You haven't told him of my—of my baby? I couldn't bear to hurt him as much as that."

"I told him that you coughed blood yesterday. He'll see you presently: he's dreadfully unhappy. He considers that, in view of your bad health, the engagement is broken by your wish—and he accepts your decision; but if he weakens, or if you weaken, I can do nothing for you or for little Tina. For heaven's sake, remember that."

Delia released her hold, and Charlotte leaned back silent, with closed eyes. On a chair near the bed lay the poplin with red velvet ribbons which had been made over in honor of her betrothal. A pair of new slippers of bronze kid peeped from beneath its folds. Poor Chatty! She had hardly had time to be pretty.

Delia sat by the bed motionless, her eyes on the closed face. They followed the course of two tears that forced a way between Charlotte's tight lids, hung on the lashes, glittered slowly down the cheeks. As the tears reached Chatty's lips, she spoke.

"Shall I live with her somewhere, do you mean? Just she and I?"

"Just you and she."

"In a little house?"

"In a little house."

"You're sure, Delia?"

"Sure, my dearest."

Charlotte once more raised herself on her elbow and slipped a hand under her pillow. She drew out a narrow ribbon on which hung a diamond luster ring.

"I had taken it off already," she said, and handed it to Delia.

CHAPTER VI

Everyone agreed afterward that you could always have told that Charlotte Lovell was meant to be an old maid. Even before her illness, it had been manifest: there was something prim about her, in spite of her fiery hair. Lucky enough for her, poor girl, considering her wretched health in her youth: Mrs. James Ralston's contemporaries, for instance, remembered Charlotte as a mere ghost, coughing her lungs out—that, of course, had been the reason for breaking her engagement with Joe Ralston.

True, she had recovered very rapidly, in spite of the peculiar treatment she was given. The Lovells, as everyone knew, couldn't afford to send her to Italy; so she was packed off to a farmhouse on the Hudson—a little place on the James Ralstons' property—where she lived for five or six years with an Irish servant-woman and a foundling baby. The story of the foundling was another queer episode in Charlotte's history. From the time of her first illness, when she was only twenty-two or -three, she had developed an almost morbid tenderness for children, especially for the children of the poor. It was said—Dr. Lanskell was understood to have said—that the baffled instinct of motherhood was peculiarly intense in cases where lung-disease prevented marriage. And so, when the Doctor decided that Chatty must break her engagement to Jim Ralston and go to live in the country, the Doctor had told her family that the only hope of saving her lay in not separating her entirely from her poor children, but in letting her choose one of them, the youngest and most pitiable, and devote herself to its care. So the James Ralstons had lent her their little farmhouse; and Mrs. Jim, with her extraordinary gift of taking things in at a glance, had at once arranged everything, and even pledged herself to look after the baby if Charlotte died.

Charlotte did not die till long afterward. She lived to grow robust and middle-aged, energetic and even tyrannical. And as the transformation in her character took place, she became more and more like the typical old maid: precise, methodical, absorbed in trifles, and attaching an exaggerated importance to the smallest social and domestic observances. Such was her reputation as a vigilant housewife that when poor Jim Ralston was killed by a fall from his horse, and left Delia, still young, with a boy and girl to bring up, it seemed perfectly natural that the heartbroken widow should take her cousin to live with her and share her task.

But Delia Ralston never did things quite like other people. When she took Charlotte, she took Charlotte's foundling too—a little dark-haired girl with pale brown eyes, and the odd incisive manner of children who have lived too much alone. The little girl was called Tina Lovell: it was vaguely supposed that Charlotte had adopted her. She grew up on terms of affectionate equality with her young Ralston cousins, and almost as much so—it might be said—with the two women who mothered her. But, by a natural instinct of imitation which no one thought it necessary to correct, she always called Delia Ralston "Mamma," and Charlotte Lovell "Aunt Chatty." She was a brilliant and engaging creature, and people marveled at poor Chatty's luck in having chosen so interesting a specimen among her foundlings—for she was by this time supposed to have had a whole asylumful to choose from.

The agreeable elderly bachelor, Sillerton Jackson, returning from a prolonged sojourn in Paris (where he was understood to have been made much of by the highest personages), pronounced himself immensely struck with Tina's charms when he saw her at her coming-out ball, and asked Delia's permission to come some evening and dine alone with her and her young people. He complimented the widow on the rosy beauty of her own young Delia; but the mother's keen eye perceived that all the while he was watching Tina, and after dinner he confided to the older ladies that there was something "very French" in the girl's way of doing her hair, and that in the capital of all the elegances she would have been pronounced extremely stylish.

"Oh—" Delia deprecated beamingly, while Charlotte

Lovell sat bent over her work with pinched lips; but Tina, who had been laughing with her cousins at the other end of the room, was around upon her elders in a flash.

"I heard what Mr. Sillerton said! Yes, I did, Mamma: he says I do my hair stylishly. Didn't I always tell you so? I *know* it's more becoming to let it curl as it wants to than to plaster it down with bandoline like Aunty's—"

"Tina, Tina—you always think people are admiring you!" Miss Lovell protested.

"Why shouldn't I, when they do?" the girl laughingly challenged; and turning her mocking eyes on Sillerton Jackson: "Do tell Aunt Charlotte not to be so dreadfully old-maidish!"

Delia saw the blood rise to Charlotte Lovell's face. It no longer painted two brick-rose circles on her thin cheek-bones, but diffused a harsh flush over her whole countenance, from the collar fastened with an old-fashioned garnet brooch to the pepper-and-salt hair (with no trace of red left in it) flattened down over her hollow temples.

That evening, when they went up to bed, Delia called Tina into her room.

"You ought not to speak to your Aunt Charlotte as you did just now, dear. It's disrespectful—and it hurts her."

The girl overflowed with compunction. "Oh, I'm so sorry! Because I said she was an old maid? But she *is*, isn't she, Mamma? In her inmost soul, I mean. I don't believe she's ever been young—ever thought of fun or admiration or falling in love—do you? That's why she never understands me, and you always do, you darling dear Mamma." With one of her light movements Tina was in the widow's arms.

"Child, child!" Delia softly scolded, kissing the dark curls planted in five points on the girl's forehead.

There was a footfall in the passage, and Charlotte Lovell stood in the doorway. Delia, without moving, gave her a glance of welcome over Tina's shoulder.

"Come in, Charlotte. I'm scolding this child for behaving like a spoiled baby before Sillerton Jackson. What will he think of her?"

"Just what she deserves, probably," Charlotte returned with a cold smile. Tina went toward her, she kissed the girl's proffered forehead just where Delia's warm lips had touched it. "Good night, child," she said, in her dry tone of dismissal.

The door closed on the two women, and Delia signed to Charlotte to take the armchair opposite her own.

"Not so near the fire," Miss Lovell answered. She chose a straight-backed chair, and sat down with folded hands. Delia's eyes rested absently on the thin, ringless hands: she wondered why Charlotte never wore her mother's jewels.

"I heard what you were saying to Tina, Delia. You were scolding her because she called me an old maid."

It was Delia's turn to color. "I scolded her for being disrespectful, dear; if you heard what I said, you can't think that I was too severe."

"Not too severe: no. I've never thought you too severe with Tina: on the contrary."

"You think I spoil her?"

"Sometimes."

Delia felt an unreasoning resentment. "What was it I said that you object to?"

Charlotte returned her glance steadily. "I would rather she thought me an old maid than—"

"Oh—" Delia murmured. With one of her quick leaps of intuition, she had entered into the other's soul, and measured its shuddering loneliness.

"What else," Charlotte inexorably pursued, "*can* she possibly be allowed to think me—ever?"

"I see—I see—" the widow faltered.

"A ridiculous, narrow-minded old maid—nothing else," Charlotte Lovell insisted, getting to her feet, "or I shall never feel safe with her."

"Good night, my dear," Delia said compassionately. There were moments when she almost hated Charlotte for being Tina's mother, and others, such as this, when her heart was wrung by the tragic spectacle of that unavowed bond.

Charlotte seemed to have divined her thought.

"Oh, but don't pity me! She's mine," she murmured, going.

CHAPTER VII

Delia Ralston sometimes felt that the real events of her life did not begin until both her children had contracted—ever so safely and suitably—the usual irreproachable New York alliances. The boy had married first, choosing a Vandergrave in whose father's bank at Albany he was to have an immediate junior partnership; and young Delia (as her mother had foreseen she would) had selected John Junius, the safest and soundest of the many young Halseys, and followed him to his parents' house the year after her brother's marriage.

After young Delia left the house in Gramercy Park, it was inevitable that Tina should take the center front of its narrow stage. Tina had reached the marriageable age; she was admired and sought after; but what hope was there of her finding a husband? The two watchful women did not propound this question to each other; but Delia Ralston, brooding over it day by day, and taking it up with her when she mounted at night to her old-fashioned bedroom, knew that Charlotte Lovell, at the same hour, carried the same problem with her to the floor above.

The two cousins, during their eight years of life together, had seldom openly disagreed. Indeed, it might almost have been said that there was nothing open in their relation. Delia would have had it otherwise: after they had once looked so deeply into each other's souls, it seemed unnatural that a veil should fall between them. But she understood that Tina's ignorance of her origin must at all costs be preserved, and that Charlotte Lovell, abrupt, passionate, and inarticulate, knew of no other security than to wall herself up in perpetual silence.

So far had she carried this self-imposed reticence that Mrs. Ralston was surprised at her suddenly asking, soon after young Delia's marriage, to be allowed to move down into the small bedroom next to Tina's, left vacant by the bride's departure.

"But you'll be so much less comfortable there, Chatty. Have you thought of that? Or is it on account of the stairs?"

"No; it's not the stairs," Charlotte answered with her usual bluntness. How could she avail herself of the pretext Delia offered her, when Delia knew that she still ran up and down the three flights like a girl? "It's because I should be next to Tina," she said, in a low voice that jarred like an untuned string.

"Oh—very well. As you please." Mrs. Ralston could not tell why she felt suddenly irritated by the request, unless it were that she had already amused herself with the idea of fitting up the vacant room as a sitting-room for Tina. She had meant to do it in pink and pale green, like an opening flower.

"Of course, if there is any reason—" Charlotte suggested, as if reading her thought.

"None whatever, except that—well, I'd meant to surprise Tina by doing the room up as a sort of little boudoir, where she could have her books and things, and see her girl friends."

"You're too kind, Delia; but Tina mustn't have boudoirs," Miss Lovell answered ironically, the green specks showing in her eyes.

"Very well: as you please," Delia repeated in the same

irritated tone. "I'll have your things brought down tomorrow."

Charlotte paused in the doorway. "You're sure there's no other reason?"

"Other reason? Why should there be?" The two women looked at each other almost with hostility, and Charlotte turned to go.

The talk once over, Delia was annoyed with herself for having yielded to Charlotte's wish. Why must it always be she who gave in, she who, after all, was the mistress of the house, and to whom both Charlotte and Tina might almost be said to owe their very existence, or at least all that made it worth having? Yet whenever any question arose about the girl, it was invariably Charlotte who gained her point, Delia who yielded: it was as if Charlotte, in her mute, obstinate way, were determined to take every advantage of the dependence that made it impossible for a woman of Delia's nature to oppose her.

In truth, Delia had looked forward more than she knew to the quiet talks with Tina to which the little boudoir would have lent itself. While her own daughter inhabited the room, Mrs. Ralston had been in the habit of spending an hour there every evening, chatting with the two girls while they undressed, and listening to their comments on the incidents of the day. She always knew beforehand exactly what her own girl would say; but Tina's views and opinions were a perpetual delicious shock to her. Not that they were unfamiliar: there were moments when they seemed to well straight up from the dumb depths of her own past. Only they expressed feelings she had never uttered, ideas she had hardly avowed to herself: Tina sometimes said things which Delia Ralston, in far-off self-communions, had imagined herself saying to Clem Spender.

And now there would be an end to these evening talks: if Charlotte had asked to be lodged next to her daughter, might it not conceivably be because she wished them to end? It had never before occurred to Delia that her influence over Tina might be resented: now it flashed a light far down into the abyss which had always divided the two women. But a moment later Delia reproached herself for attributing feelings of jealousy to her cousin. Was it not rather to herself that she should have ascribed them? Charlotte, as Tina's mother, had every right to wish to be near her, near her in all senses of the word: what claim had Delia to oppose to that natural privilege? Next morning she ordered that Charlotte's things be taken down to the room next to Tina's.

That evening, when bedtime came, Charlotte and Tina went upstairs together; but Delia lingered in the drawing-room on the pretext of having letters to write. In truth, she dreaded to pass the threshold where, evening after evening, the fresh laughter of the two girls had waylaid her, while Charlotte Lovell already slept her old-maid sleep on the floor above. It sent a pang through Delia to think that henceforth she would be cut off from this means of keeping her hold on Tina.

An hour later, when she mounted the stairs in her turn, she was guiltily conscious of moving as noiselessly as she could along the heavy carpet of the corridor, and of pausing longer than was necessary over the extinguishing of the gas-jet on the landing. As she stood there she strained her ears for the sound of voices from the doors behind which Charlotte and Tina slept; she would have been secretly hurt at hearing talk and laughter from within. But none came to her; nor was there any light beneath the doors. Evidently Charlotte, in her hard, methodical way, had said good night to her daughter on reaching her room, and gone straight to bed as usual. Perhaps she had never approved of Tina's vigils, of the long undressing punctuated with mirth and confidences; it was not unlikely, Delia reflected, that she had asked to have the room next to her daughter's simply because she wished the girl not to miss her "beauty sleep."

Whenever Delia tried to explore the secret of her cousin's actions, she returned from the adventure humiliated and abashed by the base motives she attributed to Charlotte. How was it that she, Delia Ralston, whose happiness had been open and avowed to the world, so often found herself denying poor Charlotte the secret of her scanted mother-hood? She hated herself for this moment of envy whenever she detected it, and tried to atone for it by a softened manner and a more anxious consideration for Charlotte's feelings; but the attempt was not always successful, and Delia some-times wondered if Charlotte did not resent any too open show of sympathy as an indirect glance at her misfortune.

The worst of suffering such as hers was that it left one sore to the gentlest touch.

Delia, slowly undressing before the same lace-draped toilet-glass which had reflected her bridal image, was turning over these thoughts when she heard a faint knock on her door. On the threshold stood Tina in a dressing-gown, her dark curls falling over her shoulders. With a happy heartbeat Delia held out her arms.

"I had to say good night, Mamma," the girl whispered.

"Of course, dear." Delia kissed her lifted forehead. "But run off now, or you might disturb your aunt. You know she sleeps badly, and you must be as quiet as a mouse now she's next to you."

"Yes, I know," Tina acquiesced, with a grave glance that was almost of complicity.

She asked no further question; she did not linger; lifting Delia's hand, she held it a moment against her cheek, and then stole out as noiselessly as she had come.

CHAPTER VIII

"But you must see," Charlotte Lovell insisted, laying aside the *Evening Post*, "that Tina has changed. You do see that?"

The two women were sitting alone by the drawing-room fire in Gramercy Park. Tina had gone to dine with her cousin, Delia Halsey, and was to be taken afterward to a ball at the Vandergraves', from which the John Juniuses had promised to see her home. Mrs. Ralston and Charlotte, their early dinner finished, had the long evening to themselves. It was their custom, on such occasions, for Charlotte to read the news aloud to her cousin, while the latter embroidered; but tonight, all through Charlotte's conscientious progress from column to column, without a slip or an omission, Delia had felt her, for some special reason, alert to take advantage of her daughter's absence.

To gain time, Mrs. Ralston bent over a dropped stitch in her delicate white embroidery.

"Tina changed? Since when?" she questioned.

The answer flashed out instantly. "Since Lanning Halsey has been coming here so much."

"Lanning? I used to think he came for Delia," Mrs. Ralston mused, speaking at random to gain still more time.

"It's natural you should suppose that everyone came for Delia," Charlotte rejoined dryly; "but as Lanning continues to seek every chance of being with Tina—"

Mrs. Ralston stole a swift glance at her cousin. She had in truth noticed that Tina had changed, as a flower changes at the mysterious moment when the unopened petals flush from within. The girl had grown handsomer, shyer, more silent, at times more irrelevantly gay. But Delia had not associated these variations of mood with the presence of Lanning Halsey, one of the numerous youths who had haunted the house before young Delia's marriage. There had, indeed, been a moment when Mrs. Ralston's eyes had been fixed, with a certain apprehension, on the handsome Lanning.

Among all the sturdy and stolid Halsey cousins he was the only one to whom a prudent mother might have hesitated to entrust her daughter: it would have been hard to say why, except that he was handsomer and more talkative than the rest, chronically unpunctual, and totally unperturbed by the fact. Clem Spender had been like that; and what if young Delia—?

But young Delia's mother was speedily reassured. The girl, herself arch and appetizing, took no interest in the corresponding graces except when backed by more solid qualities. A Ralston to the core, she demanded the Ralston virtues, and chose the Halsey most worthy of a Ralston bride.

Mrs. Ralston felt that Charlotte was waiting for her to speak. "It will be hard to get used to the idea of Tina's marrying," she said gently. "I don't know what we two old women shall do, alone in this empty house—for it will be an empty house then. But I suppose we ought to face the idea."

"I *do* face it," said Charlotte Lovell gravely.

"And you dislike Lanning? I mean as a husband for Tina?"

Miss Lovell folded the evening paper and stretched out a thin hand for her knitting. She glanced across the citron-wood work-table at her cousin. "Tina must not be too difficult—" she began.

"Oh—" Delia protested, reddening.

"Let us call things by their names," the other evenly pursued. "That's my way, when I speak at all. Usually, as you know, I say nothing."

The widow made a sign of assent and Charlotte went on: "It's better so. But I've always known a time would come when we should have to talk things out."

"Talk things out? You and I? What things?"

"Tina's future."

There was a silence. Delia Ralston, who always respond-ed instantly to the least appeal to her sincerity, breathed a deep sigh of relief. At last the ice in Charlotte's breast was breaking up!

"My dear," Delia murmured, "you know how much Tina's happiness concerns me. If you disapprove of Lanning Halsey as a husband, have you any other candidate in mind?"

Miss Lovell smiled one of her faint hard smiles. "I am not aware that there is a queue at the door. Nor do I disapprove of Lanning Halsey as a husband. Personally, I find him very agreeable: I understand his attraction for Tina."

"Ah—Tina *is* attracted?"

"Yes."

Mrs. Ralston pushed aside her work and thoughtfully considered her cousin's sharply lined face. Never had Char-lotte Lovell more completely presented the typical image of the old maid than as she sat there, upright on her straight-backed chair, with narrowed elbows and clicking needles, and imperturbably discussed her daughter's marriage.

"I don't understand, Chatty. Whatever Lanning's faults are—and I don't believe they're grave—I share your liking for him. After all"—Mrs. Ralston paused—"what is it that people find so reprehensible in him? Chiefly, as far as I can hear, that he can't decide on the choice of a profession. The New York view about that is rather narrow, as we know. Young men may have other tastes—artistic—literary; they may even have difficulty in deciding."

Both women colored slightly, and Delia guessed that the same reminiscence which shook her own bosom also throbbed under Charlotte's straitened bodice.

Charlotte spoke. "Yes: I understand that. But hesitancy about a profession may cause hesitancy about—other decisions."

"What do you mean? Surely not that Lanning—?"

"Lanning has not asked Tina to marry him."

"And you think he's hesitating?"

Charlotte paused. The steady click of her needles punctuated the silence as once, years before, it had been punctuated by the tick of the Parisian clock on Delia's mantel. As Delia's memory fled back to that scene, she felt its mysterious tension in the air.

Charlotte spoke. "Lanning is not hesitating any longer: he has decided not to marry Tina. But he has also decided—not to give up seeing her."

Delia flushed abruptly: she was irritated and bewildered by Charlotte's oracular phrases, doled out between parsimonious lips.

"You don't mean that he has offered himself and then drawn back? I can't think him capable of such an insult to Tina."

"He has not insulted Tina. He has simply told her that he can't afford to marry. Until he chooses a profession, his father will allow him only a few hundred dollars a year; and that may be suppressed if—if he marries against his parents' wishes."

It was Delia's turn to be silent. The past was too over-whelmingly resuscitated in Charlotte's words. Clement Spender stood before her, irresolute, impecunious, persuasive. Ah, if only she had let herself be persuaded!

"I'm very sorry that this should have happened to Tina. But as Lanning appears to have behaved honorably, and withdrawn without raising false expectations, we must hope—we must hope—" Delia paused, not knowing what they must hope.

Charlotte Lovell laid down her knitting. "You know as well as I do, Delia, that every young man who is attracted by Tina will find as good reasons for not marrying her."

"Then you think his withdrawal a pretext?"

"Naturally. The first of many that will be found by his successors—for of course he will have successors. Tina—attracts."

"Ah," Delia murmured.

Here they were at last face to face with the problem which, through all the years of silence and evasiveness, had lain as close to the surface as a body too hastily concealed! Delia drew another deep breath, which again was almost one of relief. She had always known that it would be difficult, almost impossible, to find a husband for Tina; and much as she desired Tina's happiness, some inmost selfishness whispered how much less lonely and purposeless the close of her own life would be should the girl be forced to share it. But how say this to Tina's mother?

"I hope you exaggerate, Charlotte. There may be disinterested characters. But, in any case, surely Tina need not be unhappy here, with us who love her so dearly."

"Tina an old maid? Never!" Charlotte Lovell rose abruptly, her closed hand crashing down on the slender work-table. "My child shall have her life—her own life— whatever it costs me."

Delia's ready sympathy welled up. "I understand your feeling. I should want also—hard as it will be to let her go. But surely there is no hurry—no reason for looking so far ahead. The child is not twenty. Wait."

Charlotte stood before her, motionless, perpendicular. At such moments she made Delia think of lava struggling through granite: there seemed no issue for the fires within.

"Wait? But if *she* doesn't wait?"

"But if he has withdrawn—what do you mean?"

"He has given up marrying her—but not seeing her."

Delia sprang up in her turn, flushed and trembling.

"Charlotte! Do you know what you are insinuating?"

"Yes: I know."

"But it's too outrageous. No decent girl—"

The words died on Delia's lips. Charlotte Lovell held her eyes inexorably. "Girls are not always what you call decent," she declared.

Mrs. Ralston turned slowly back to her seat. Her tambour frame had fallen to the floor: she stooped heavily to pick it up. Charlotte hung over her, relentless as doom.

"I can't imagine, Charlotte, what is gained by saying such things—even by hinting them. Surely you trust your own child—"

Charlotte laughed. "My mother trusted me," she said.

"How dare you—how dare you?" Delia began; but her eyes fell, and she felt a tremor of weakness in her throat.

"Oh, I dare anything for Tina, even to judging her as she is," Tina's mother murmured.

"As she is? She's perfect."

"Let us say, then, that she must pay for my imperfections. All I want is that she shouldn't pay too heavily."

Mrs. Ralston sat silent. It seemed to her that Charlotte spoke with the voice of all the dark destinies coiled under the safe surface of life; and that to such a voice there was no answer but an awed acquiescence.

"Poor Tina!" she breathed.

"Oh, I don't mean that she shall suffer! It's not for that that I've waited—waited. Only I've made mistakes: mistakes that I understand now, and must remedy. You've been too good to us—and we must go."

"Go?" Delia gasped.

"Yes. Don't think me ungrateful. You saved my child once—do you suppose I can forget? But now it's my turn—it's I who must save her. And it's only by taking her away from everything here—from everything she's known till now—that I can do it. She's lived too long among unrealities: and she's like me. They won't content her!"

"Unrealities?" Delia echoed vaguely.

"Unrealities for her. Young men who make love to her and can't marry her. Happy households where she's welcomed till she's suspected of designs on a brother or a husband—or else exposed to their insults. How could we ever have imagined, either of us, that the child could escape disaster? I thought only of her present happiness—of all the advantages, for both of us, of being with you. But this affair with young Halsey has opened my eyes. I must take Tina away. We must go and live somewhere where we're not known, where we shall be among plain people, leading plain lives. Somewhere where she can find a husband, and make herself a home."

Charlotte paused. She had spoken in a rapid, monotonous tone, as if by rote; but now her voice broke, and she repeated painfully: "I'm not ungrateful."

"Oh, don't let's speak of gratitude! What place has it between you and me?"

Delia had risen and begun to move uneasily about the room. She longed to plead with Charlotte, to implore her not to be in haste, to picture to her the cruelty of severing Tina from all her habits and associations, of carrying her inexplicably away to lead "a plain life among plain people." What chance was there, indeed, that a creature so radiant could tamely submit to such a fate, or find an acceptable husband in such conditions? The change might only precipitate a tragedy. Delia's experience was too limited for her to picture exactly what might happen to a girl like Tina, suddenly cut off from all that sweetened life for her; but vague visions of revolt and flight—of a "fall" deeper and more irretrievable than Charlotte's—flashed through her agonized imagination.

"It's too cruel—it's too cruel," she cried, speaking to herself rather than to Charlotte.

Charlotte, instead of answering, glanced abruptly at the clock.

"Do you know what time it is? Past midnight! I mustn't keep you sitting up for my foolish girl."

Delia's heart contracted. She saw that Charlotte wished to cut the conversation short, and to do so by reminding her that only Tina's mother had a right to decide what Tina's future should be. At that moment, though Delia had just protested that there could be no question of gratitude between them, Charlotte Lovell seemed to her a monster of ingratitude, and it was on the tip of her tongue to cry out: "Have all the years then given me no share in Tina?" But at the same instant she had put herself once more in Charlotte's place, and was feeling the mother's fierce terrors for her child. It was natural enough that Charlotte should resent the faintest attempt to usurp in private the authority she could never assert in public. With a pang of compassion Delia realized that she was literally the one being on earth before whom Charlotte could act the mother. "Poor thing—ah, let her!" she murmured inwardly.

"But why should you sit up for Tina? She has the key, and Delia is to bring her home."

Charlotte Lovell did not immediately answer. She rolled up her knitting, looked severely at one of the candelabra on the mantelpiece, and crossed over to straighten it. Then she picked up her work-bag.

"Yes, as you say—why should anyone sit up for her?" She moved about the room, blowing out the lamps, covering the fire, assuring herself that the windows were bolted, while Delia passively watched her. Then the cousins lighted their candles and walked upstairs through the darkened house. Charlotte seemed determined to make no further allusion to the subject of their talk. On the landing she paused, bending her head toward Delia's nightly kiss.

"I hope they've kept up your fire," she said, with her capable housekeeping air; and on Delia's hasty reassurance, the two murmured a simultaneous "Good night," and Charlotte turned down the passage to her room.

CHAPTER IX

Delia's fire had been kept up, and her dressing-gown was warming on an armchair near the hearth. But she neither undressed nor yet seated herself. Her conversation with Charlotte had filled her with a deep unrest.

For a few moments she stood in the middle of the floor, looking slowly about her. Nothing had ever been changed in the room which, even as a bride, she had planned to modernize. All her dreams of renovation had faded long ago. Some deep central indifference had gradually made her regard herself as a third person, living the life meant for another woman, a woman totally unrelated to the vivid Delia Lovell who had entered that house so full of plans and visions. The fault, she knew, was not her husband's. With a little managing and a little wheedling, she would have gained every point as easily as she had gained the capital one of taking the foundling baby under her wing. The difficulty was that, after that victory, nothing else seemed worth trying for. The first sight of little Tina had somehow decentralized Delia Ralston's whole life, making her indifferent to everything else, except indeed the welfare of her own husband and children. Ahead of her she saw only a future full of duties, and these she had gayly and faithfully accomplished. But her own life was over: she felt as detached as a cloistered nun. The change in her was too deep not to be visible. The Ralstons openly gloried in dear Delia's conformity. Each acquiescence passed for a concession, and their doctrine was fortified by such fresh proofs of its durability. Now, as Delia glanced about her at the Leopold Robert lithographs, the family daguerreotypes, the rosewood and mahogany, she understood that she was looking at the walls of her own grave.

The change had come on the day when Charlotte Lovell, cowering on that very lounge, had made her terrible avowal. Then for the first time Delia, with a kind of fearful exaltation, had heard the blind forces of life groping and crying underfoot. But that day also she had known herself excluded from them, doomed to dwell among shadows. Life had passed her by, and left her with the Ralstons.

Very well, then! She would make the best of herself, and of the Ralstons. The vow was immediate and unflinching; and for nearly twenty years she had gone on observing it. Once only had she been not a Ralston but herself; once only had it seemed worth while. And now perhaps the same challenge had sounded again; again, for a moment, it might be worth while to live. Not for the sake of Clement Spender —poor Clement, married years ago to a plain determined cousin, who had hunted him down in Rome, and inclosing him in an unrelenting domesticity, had obliged all New York on the grand tour to buy his pictures with a resigned grimace. No, not for Clement Spender, hardly for Charlotte or Tina; but for her own sake, hers, Delia Ralston's, for the sake of her one missed vision, her forfeited reality, she would once more break down the Ralston barriers and reach out into the world.

A faint sound through the silent house disturbed Delia Ralston's meditation. Listening, she heard Charlotte Lovell's door open, and her stiff petticoats rustle toward the landing. A light glanced under the door and vanished; Charlotte had passed the threshold on her way downstairs.

Without moving, Delia continued to listen. Perhaps the careful Charlotte had gone down to make sure that the front door was not bolted, or that she had really covered up the fire. In that case, her step would presently be heard returning. But no step sounded; and it became gradually evident that Charlotte had gone downstairs to wait for her daughter. Why?

Delia's room was at the front of the house. She stole across the heavy carpet, drew aside the curtains, and cautiously folded back the inner shutters. Below her lay the empty square, white with moonlight, its tree-trunks patterned on a fresh sprinkling of snow. The houses opposite slept in darkness: not a footstep broke the white surface; not a wheel-track marred the brilliant street. Overhead a heaven full of stars swam in the moonlight.

Of the households around Gramercy Park Delia knew that only two others had gone to the ball: the Petrus Vandergraves and their cousins, the young Parmly Ralstons. The Lucius Lannings had just entered on their three years of mourning for Mrs. Lucius's mother (it was hard on their daughter Kate, just eighteen, who would be unable to "come out" till she was twenty-one); young Mrs. Marcy Mingott was "expecting her third," and consequently secluded from the public eye for nearly a year; and the other denizens of the Square belonged to the undifferentiated and uninvited.

Delia pressed her forehead against the pane. Before long, carriages would turn the corner, and the sleeping square ring with hoof-beats; fresh laughter and young farewells would mount from the door-steps. But why was Charlotte waiting for her daughter downstairs in the darkness?

The Parisian clock struck one. Delia came back into the room, raked the fire, picked up a shawl, and wrapped in it, returned to her vigil. Ah, how old she must have grown, that she should feel the cold at such a moment! It reminded her of what the future held for her: neuralgia, rheumatism, stiffness, accumulating infirmities. And never had she kept a moonlight watch with a lover's arms to warm her.

The square still lay silent. Yet the ball must surely be ending: the gayest dances did not last long after one in the morning, and the drive from University Place to Gramercy Park was a short one. Delia leaned in the embrasure and listened.

Hoof-beats sounded in Irving Place, and the Petrus Vandergraves' family coach drew up before the opposite house. The Vandergrave girls and their brother sprang out and mounted the steps; then the coach stopped a few doors farther on, and the Parmly Ralstons, brought home by their cousins, descended at their own door. The next carriage that rounded the corner must therefore be the John Juniuses', bringing Tina.

The gilt clock struck half-past one. Delia wondered, knowing that young Delia, out of regard for John Junius's business hours, never stayed late at evening parties. Doubtless Tina had delayed her; Mrs. Ralston felt a little annoyed with Tina's thoughtlessness in keeping her cousin up. But the feeling was swept away by an immediate wave of sympathy. "We must go away somewhere, and lead plain lives among plain people." If Charlotte had carried out her threat—and Delia knew she would hardly have spoken unless her resolve had been taken—it might be that at that very moment poor Tina was dancing her last *valse*.

Another quarter of an hour passed; then, just as the cold was penetrating Delia's shawl, she saw two people turn into the deserted square from Irving Place. One was a young man in beaver hat and ample cloak. To his arm clung a feminine figure so closely wrapped and muffled that, until the corner light fell on it, Delia hesitated. After that, she wondered that she had not at once recognized Tina's dancing step, and her manner of tilting her head a little sideways to look up at the person she was talking to.

Tina—Tina and Lanning Halsey, walking home alone in the small hours from the Vandergrave ball! Delia's first thought was of an accident: the carriage might have broken down, or her daughter been taken ill and obliged to return home. But no: in the latter case she would have sent the carriage on with Tina. And if there had been an accident of any sort, the young people would have been hastening to apprise Mrs. Ralston; instead of which, through the bitter brilliant night, they sauntered like lovers in a midsummer glade, and Tina's thin slippers might have been treading daisies instead of snow.

Delia began to tremble like a girl. In a flash she had the answer to a question which had long been the subject of her secret conjectures. How did lovers like Charlotte and Clement Spender contrive to met? What Latmian solitude hid their clandestine joys? In the exposed compact little society to which they all belonged, how was it possible, literally—for such things to happen? Delia would never have dared to put the question to Charlotte; there were moments when she almost preferred not to know, not even to hazard a guess. But now, at a glance, she understood. How often Charlotte Lovell, staying alone in town with her infirm grandmother, must have walked home from evening parties with Clement Spender, how often have let herself and him into the darkened house in Mercer Street, where there was no one to spy upon their coming but a deaf old lady and her aged servants, all securely sleeping overhead! Delia, at the thought, saw the grim drawing-room which had been their moonlit forest, the drawing-room into which old Mrs. Lovell no longer descended, with its swathed chandelier and hard Empire sofas, and the blank-faced caryatids of the mantel; she pictured the shaft of moonlight falling across the swans and garlands of the pompous carpet, and in that icy light two young figures in each other's arms.

Yes: It must have been some such memory that had roused Charlotte's suspicions, excited her fears, sent her down in the darkness to confront the culprits. Delia shivered at the irony of the confrontation. If Tina had but known! But to Tina, of course, Charlotte was still what she had long since resolved to be: the image of prudish spinsterhood. And Delia could imagine how quietly and decently the scene below stairs would presently be enacted: no astonishment, no reproaches, no insinuations, but a smiling and resolute ignoring of excuses.

"What, Tina? You walked home with Lanning? You

imprudent child—in this wet snow! Ah, I see: Delia was worried about the baby, and ran off early, promising to send back the carriage—and it never came? Well, my dear, I congratulate you on finding Lanning to see you home. . . . Yes—I sat up because I couldn't for the life of me remember whether you'd taken the latch-key—was there ever such a flighty old aunt? But don't tell your mamma, dear, or she'd scold me for being so forgetful, and for staying downstairs in the cold. . . . You're quite sure you have the key? Ah, Lanning has it? Thank you, Lanning—so kind! Good night—or one really ought to say, good morning!"

As Delia reached this point in her mute representation of Charlotte's monologue, the front door slammed below, and young Lanning Halsey walked slowly away across the square. Delia saw him pause on the opposite pavement, look up at the unlit house-front, and then turn lingeringly away. His dismissal had taken exactly as long as Delia had calculated it would. A moment later she saw a passing light under her door, heard the starched rustle of Charlotte's petticoats, and knew that mother and daughter had reached their rooms.

Slowly, with stiff motions, she began to undress, blew out her candles, and knelt long by her bedside, her face hidden.

CHAPTER X

Lying awake till morning, Delia lived over every detail of the fateful day when she had assumed the charge of Charlotte's child. At the time she had been hardly more than a child herself, and then there had been no one for her to turn to, no one to fortify her resolution, or to advise her how to put it into effect. Since then, the accumulated experiences of seventeen years ought to have prepared her for emergencies, and taught her to advise others instead of seeking their guidance. But these years of experience weighed on her like chains binding her down to her narrow plot of life: independent action struck her as more dangerous, less conceivable, than when she had first ventured on it. There seemed to be so many more people to "consider" now ("consider" was the Ralston word): her children, their children, the families into which they had married. What would the Halseys say, and what the Ralstons? Had she then become a Ralston through and through?

A few hours later she sat in old Dr. Lanskell's library, her eyes on his sooty Smyrna rug. Dr. Lanskell no longer practiced: at most, he went to a few old patients, gave consultations in "difficult" cases. But he remained a power in his own kingdom, a sort of lay pope or medical elder, to whom the patients he had healed of physical ills now returned for moral medicine. People were agreed that Dr. Lanskell's judgment was sound; but what secretly drew them to him was the fact that, in the most totem-ridden of communities he was known not to be afraid of anything.

Now, as Delia sat by his grate, and watched his massive silver-headed figure moving ponderously about the room, between rows of calf bindings and the Dying Gladiators and

Young Augustuses of grateful patients, she already felt the reassurance communicated by his mere bodily presence.

"You see, when I first took Tina, I didn't perhaps consider sufficiently—"

The Doctor halted behind his desk and brought his fist down on it in a genial thump. "Thank God you didn't! There are considerers enough in this town without you, Delia Lovell."

She looked up quickly. "Why do you call me Delia Lovell?"

"Well, because today I rather suspect you *are*," he rejoined astutely; and she met this with a wistful laugh.

"Perhaps, if I hadn't been, once before—I mean, if I'd always been a prudent deliberate Ralston, it would have been kinder to Tina in the end."

Dr. Lanskell sank his gouty bulk into the chair behind his desk, and beamed at her through ironic spectacles. "I hate in-the-end kindnesses: they're about as nourishing as the third day of cold mutton."

She pondered. "Of course I realize that if I adopt Tina—"

"Yes?"

"Well, people will say—" A deep blush rose to her throat, covered her cheeks and brow, and ran like fire under her decently parted hair.

He nodded: "Yes."

"Or else—" the blush darkened—"that she's Jim's—"

Again Dr. Lanskell nodded. "That's what they're more likely to think; and what's the harm if they do? I know Jim:

he asked no questions when you took the child—but he knew whose she was."

She raised astonished eyes. "He knew?"

"Yes: he came to me. And—well—in the baby's interest, I violated professional secrecy. That's how Tina got a home. You're not going to denounce me, are you?"

"Oh, Dr. Lanskell!" Her eyes filled with painful tears. "Jim knew? And didn't tell me?"

"No. People didn't tell each other things much in those days, did they? But he admired you enormously for what you did. And if you assume—as I suppose you do—that he's now in a world of completer enlightenment, why not take it for granted that he'll admire you still more for what you're going to do? Presumably," the Doctor concluded sardonically, "people realize in heaven that it's a devilish sight harder, on earth, to do a brave thing at fifty than at twenty-five."

"Ah, that's what I was thinking this morning," she confessed.

"Well, you're going to prove the contrary this afternoon." He looked at his watch, stood up, and laid a fatherly hand on her shoulder. "Let people think what they choose; and send young Delia to me if she gives you any trouble. Your boy won't, you know, nor John Junius either; it must have been a woman who invented that third-and-fourth generation idea."

An elderly maidservant looked in, and Delia rose; but on the threshold she halted.

"I have an idea it's Charlotte I may have to send to you."

"Charlotte?"

"She'll hate what I'm going to do, you know."

Dr. Lanskell lifted his silver eyebrows. "Yes: poor Charlotte! I suppose she's jealous? That's where the truth of the third-and-fourth generation business comes in, after all. Somebody always has to foot the bill."

"Ah—if only Tina doesn't!"

"Well—that's just what Charlotte will come to recognize. So your course is clear."

He guided her out through the brown dining-room, where some poor people and one or two old patients were already waiting.

Delia's course, in truth, seemed clear enough till, that afternoon, she summoned Charlotte alone to her bedroom. Tina was lying down with a headache: it was the accepted attitude of young ladies in sentimental dilemmas, and greatly simplified the communion of their elders.

Delia and Charlotte had exchanged only conventional phrases over their midday meal; but Delia had the sense that her cousin's resolution was definitely taken. The events of the previous evening had evidently confirmed Charlotte's view that the time had come for decisive measures.

Miss Lovell, closing the bedroom door with her dry deliberateness, advanced toward the chintz lounge between the windows.

"You wanted to see me, Delia?"

"Yes—oh, don't sit there," Mrs. Ralston exclaimed uncontrollably.

Charlotte stared: was it possible that she did not remember the sobs of anguish she had once smothered in those cushions?

"Not—"

"No; come nearer. Sometimes I think I'm a little deaf," Delia nervously explained, pushing a chair up to her own.

"Ah!" Charlotte seated herself. "I hadn't remarked it. But if you are, it may have saved you from hearing at what hour of the morning Tina came back from the Vandergraves. She would never forgive herself—inconsiderate as she is—if she thought she'd waked you."

"She didn't wake me," Delia answered. Inwardly she thought: "Charlotte's mind is made up; I sha'n't be able to move her."

"I suppose Tina enjoyed herself very much at the ball?" she continued.

"Well, she's paying for it with a sick headache. Such excitements are not meant for her. I've already told you—"

"Yes," Mrs. Ralston interrupted. "It's to continue our talk that I've asked you to come up this afternoon."

"To continue it?" The brick-red circles appeared in Charlotte's dried cheeks. "Is it worth while? I think I ought to tell you at once that my mind's made up. You must recognize that I know what's best for Tina."

"Yes; of course. But won't you at least allow me a share in your decision?"

"A share?"

Delia leaned forward, laying a warm hand on her cousin's interlocked fingers. "Charlotte, once in this room you asked me to help you—you believed I could. Won't you believe it again?"

Charlotte's lips grew rigid. "I believe the time has come for me to help myself."

"At the cost of Tina's happiness?"

"No; but to spare her greater unhappiness."

"But Charlotte, Tina's happiness is all I want."

"Oh, I know. You've done all you could do for my child."

"No, not all." Delia rose, and stood before her cousin with a kind of solemnity. "But now I'm going to." It was as if she had pronounced a vow.

Charlotte looked up with a glitter of apprehension in her eyes.

"If you mean that you're going to use your influence with the Halseys—I'm very grateful to you; I shall always be grateful. But I don't want a compulsory marriage for my child."

Delia flushed at the other's incomprehension. It seemed to her that her purpose must be written on her face. "I'm going to adopt Tina—give her my name," she said.

Charlotte stared at her stonily. "Adopt her—adopt her?"

"Don't you see, dear, the difference it will make? There's

my mother's money—the Lovell money; it is not much, to be sure; but Jim always wanted it to go back to my family. And my Delia and her brother are so handsomely provided for. There's no reason why my little fortune shouldn't go to Tina—and why she shouldn't be known as Tina Ralston." Delia paused. "I believe—I think I know—that Jim would have approved of that too."

"*Approved*?"

"Yes. Can't you see that when he let me take the child, he must have foreseen and accepted whatever—might come of it?"

Charlotte stood up also. "Thank you, Delia. But nothing more must come of it, except our leaving you—our leaving you now. I'm sure that's what Jim would have approved."

Mrs. Ralston drew back a step or two. Charlotte's cold resolution benumbed her courage, and she could find no immediate reply.

"Ah, then it's easier for you to sacrifice Tina's happiness than your pride?"

"My pride? I've no right to any pride, except in my child. And that I'll never sacrifice."

"No one asks you to. You're not reasonable. You're cruel. All I want is to be allowed to help Tina, and you speak as if I were interfering with your rights."

"My rights?" Charlotte caught her up again. "What are they? I have no rights, either before the law or in the heart of my own child."

"How can you say such things? You know how Tina loves you."

"Yes—compassionately, as I used to love my old-maid aunts. There were two of them—you remember? Like withered babies! We children used to be warned never to say anything that might shock Aunt Josie or Aunt Nonie, exactly as I heard you telling Tina the other night—"

"Oh—" Delia murmured.

Charlotte Lovell stood before her, haggard, rigid, unrelenting. "No, it's gone on long enough. I mean to tell her everything—and to take her away."

"To tell her about her birth?"

"I was never ashamed of it," Charlotte panted.

"You sacrifice her, then—sacrifice her to your desire for mastery?"

The two women faced each other, both with weapons spent. Delia, through the tremor of her own indignation, saw her antagonist waver, step backward, sink down with a broken murmur on the lounge. Charlotte hid her face in the cushions, clenching them with violent hands. The same fierce maternal passion that had once flung her down upon those same cushions was now bowing her still lower, in the throes of a bitterer renunciation. Delia seemed to hear again the old cry: "But how can I give up my baby?" Her own momentary resentment melted, and she bent over the mother's laboring shoulders.

"Chatty—it won't be like giving her up this time. Can't we just go on loving her together?"

Charlotte did not answer. For a long time she lay silent, immovable, her face hidden: she seemed to fear to turn it to the face bent down to her. But presently Delia was aware of a gradual relaxing of the stretched muscles, and saw that one of her cousin's hands was stirring and groping. She lowered her hand to the seeking fingers, and it was caught and pressed to Charlotte's lips.

CHAPTER XI

Tina Lovell—now Miss Clementina Ralston—was to be married in July to Lanning Halsey. The engagement had been announced only in the previous April; and the female elders of the tribe had begun by crying out against the indelicacy of so brief a betrothal. It was unanimously agreed in New York that "young people should be given the time to get to know each other"; and though the greater number of the couples constituting New York society had played together as children, and been born of parents as long and as familiarly acquainted, yet some mysterious law of decorum required that the newly affianced should always be regarded as being also newly acquainted. In the Southern States things were differently conducted: headlong engagements, even runaway marriages, were not uncommon in the annals of Virginia and Maryland; but such rashness was less consonant with the sluggish blood of New York, where the pace of life was still set with a Dutch deliberateness.

In a case as unusual as Tina Ralston's, however, it was

hardly surprising that tradition had been disregarded. In the first place, everyone knew that she was no more Tina Ralston than you or I—unless, indeed, one were to credit the rumors about poor Jim's unsuspected "past," and his widow's magnanimity. But the opinion of the majority was against this. People were reluctant to charge a dead man with an offense from which he could not clear himself; and the Ralstons unanimously declared that, thoroughly as they disapproved of Mrs. James Ralston's action, they were convinced that she would not have adopted Tina had her doing so appeared to "cast a slur" on her late husband's morals.

No: the girl was perhaps a Lovell—though even that idea was not generally held—but she was certainly not a Ralston. Her black eyes and flighty ways too obviously excluded her from the clan for any formal excommunication to be pronounced against her. In fact, most people believed that—as Dr. Lanskell had always affirmed—her origin was really undiscoverable, that she represented one of the unsolved mysteries which occasionally perplex and irritate well-regulated societies, and that her adoption by Delia Ralston was simply one more proof of the Lovell clannishness, since the child had been taken in by Mrs. Ralston only because her cousin Charlotte was so attached to it. To say that Mrs. Ralston's son and daughter were pleased with the idea of Tina's adoption would have been an exaggeration; but they abstained from comment, minimizing the effect of their mother's whim by a dignified silence. It was the old New York way for families thus to screen the eccentricities of an individual member, and where there was "money enough to go around," the heirs would have been thought vulgarly grasping to protest at the alienation of a small sum from the general inheritance.

Nevertheless, Delia Ralston, from the moment of Tina's adoption, was perfectly aware of a different attitude on the part of her children. They dealt with her patiently, almost paternally, as with a minor in whom one juvenile lapse has been condoned, but who must be subjected, in consequence, to a stricter vigilance; and society treated her in the same indulgent but guarded manner.

She had (it was Sillerton Jackson who first phrased it) an undoubted way of "carrying things off"; since Mrs. Manson Mingott had broken her husband's will, nothing like it had been seen in New York. But Mrs. Ralston's method was different, and less easy to analyze. What Mrs. Manson Mingott had accomplished with epigram, invective, insistency, and runnings to and fro, the other achieved without raising her voice or seeming to take a step from the beaten path. When she had persuaded Jim Ralston to take in the foundling baby, it had been done in the turn of a hand, one didn't know when or how; and the next day he and she were as untroubled and beaming as usual. And now, this adoption! Well, she had pursued the same method; as Sillerton Jackson said, she behaved as if her adopting Tina had always been an understood thing, as if she wondered that people should wonder. And in face of her wonder, theirs seemed foolish, and they gradually desisted.

In reality, behind Delia's assurance there was a tumult of doubts and uncertainties. But she had once learned that one can do almost anything (perhaps even murder) if one does not attempt to explain it; and the lesson had never been forgotten. She had never explained the taking over of the foundling baby; nor was she now going to explain its adoption. She was just going about her business as if nothing had happened that needed to be accounted for; and a long inheritance of moral modesty helped her to keep her questionings to herself.

These questionings were in fact less concerned with public opinion than with Charlotte Lovell's private thoughts. Charlotte, after her first moment of tragic resistance, had shown herself pathetically, almost painfully, grateful. That she had reason to be, Tina's attitude abundantly revealed. Tina, during the first days after her return from the Vandergrave ball, had shown a closed and darkened face that terribly reminded Delia of the ghastliness of Charlotte Lovell's sudden reflection, years before, in her own bedroom mirror. The first chapter of the mother's history was already written in the daughter's eyes; and the Spender blood in Tina might well precipitate the sequence. In those few hours of silent observation Delia perceived, with terror and compassion, the justification of Charlotte's misgivings. The girl had nearly been lost to them both: at all costs such a risk must not be renewed.

The Halseys, on the whole, had behaved admirably. Lanning wished to marry dear Delia Ralston's protégée—who was shortly, it was understood, to take her adopted mother's name, and inherit her fortune. To what more could a Halsey aspire than one more alliance with a Ralston? The families had always intermarried. The Halsey parents gave their blessing with a precipitation which made it evident that they too had their anxieties, and that the relief of seeing Lanning "settled" would more than compensate for the conceivable drawbacks of the marriage—though, once it was decided on, they would not admit that such drawbacks existed. For old New York always thought away whatever interfered with the perfect propriety of its arrangements.

Charlotte Lovell of course perceived and recognized all this. She accepted the situation—in her private hours with Delia—as one more in the long list of mercies bestowed on an undeserving sinner. And one phrase of hers perhaps gave the clue to her acceptance: "Now at least she'll never suspect the truth." It had come to be the poor creature's ruling purpose that her child should never guess the tie between them.

But Delia's chief support was the sight of Tina. The older woman, whose whole life had been shaped and colored by the faint reflection of a rejected happiness, hung dazzled in the light of bliss accepted. Sometimes, as she watched Tina's changing face, she felt as though her own blood were beating in it, as though she could read every thought and emotion feeding those tumultuous currents. Tina's love was a stormy affair, with endless ups and downs of rapture and depression, arrogance and self-abasement; and Delia saw displayed before her, with an artless frankness, all the visions, cravings, and imaginings of her own stifled youth.

What the girl really thought of her adoption it was not easy to discover. She had been given, at fourteen, the current version of her origin, and had accepted it as carelessly as a happy child accepts some remote and inconceivable fact that does not alter the familiar order of things. And she accepted her adoption in the same spirit. She knew that the name of Ralston had been given to her to facilitate her marriage with Lanning Halsey; and Delia had the impression that all irrelevant questionings were submerged in an overwhelming gratitude. "I've always thought of you as my mamma; and now, you dearest, you really are," she had whispered, her cheek against Delia's; and Delia had laughed back: "Well, if the lawyers can make me so!" But there the matter dropped, swept away on the current of Tina's bliss. They were all, in those days—Delia, Charlotte, even the gallant Lanning—rather like straws whirling about on a sunlit torrent.

The golden flood swept them onward, nearer and nearer to the enchanted date; and Delia, deep in bridal preparations, wondered at the comparative indifference with which she had ordered and inspected her own daughter's twelve-dozen-of-everything. There had been nothing to quicken the pulse in young Delia's placid bridal; but as Tina's wedding-day approached, imagination burgeoned like the year. The wedding was to be celebrated at Lovell Place, the old house on the Sound where Delia Lovell had herself been married, and where, since her mother's death, she spent her summers. Although the neighborhood was already overspread with a network of mean streets, the old house, with its thin colonnaded veranda, still looked across an uncurtailed lawn and leafy shrubberies to the narrows of Hell Gate; and the drawing-rooms kept their frail, slender settees, their Sheraton consoles and cabinets. It had been thought useless to discard them for more fashionable furniture, since the growth of the city made it certain that the place must eventually be sold.

Tina, like Mrs. Ralston, was to have a "house-wedding," though Episcopalian society was beginning to disapprove of such ceremonies, which were regarded as the despised *pis aller* of Baptists, Methodists, Unitarians, and the other altarless sects. In Tina's case, however, both Delia and Charlotte felt that the greater privacy of a marriage in the house made up for its more secular character; and the Halseys discreetly favored their decision. The ladies accordingly settled themselves at Lovell Place before the end of June, and every morning young Lanning Halsey's cat-boat was seen beating across the bay, and furling its sail at the anchorage below the lawn.

There had never been a fairer June in anyone's memory. The damask roses and mignonette below the verandah had never sent such a breath of summer through the tall French windows; the gnarled orange-trees brought out from the old arcaded orange-house had never been so thickly blossomed;

the very haycocks on the lawn gave out whiffs of Araby.

The day before the wedding Delia Ralston sat on the veranda watching the moon rise across the Sound. She was tired with the multitude of last preparations, and sad at the thought of Tina's going. On the following evening the house would be empty; till death came, she and Charlotte would sit alone together beside the evening lamp. Such repinings were foolish—they were, she reminded herself, "not like her." But too many memories stirred and murmured in her: her heart was haunted. As she closed the door on the silent drawing-room—already transformed into a chapel, with its lace-hung altar, the tall alabaster vases awaiting their white roses and June lilies, the strip of red carpet dividing the rows of chairs from door to chancel—she felt that it had been a mistake to come back to Lovell Place for the wedding. She saw herself again, in her high-waisted "India mull" embroidered with daisies, her satin sandals, her Brussels veil—saw again her reflection in the sallow pier-glass, as she had entered that same room on Jim Ralston's triumphant arm, and the one terrified glance she had exchanged with her own image before she took her stand under the bell of white roses, and smiled upon the congratulating company. Ah, what a different image the pier-glass would reflect tomorrow!

Charlotte Lovell's brisk step sounded in the hall, and she came out and joined Mrs. Ralston.

"I've been to the kitchen to tell Melissa Grimes that she'd better count on two hundred plates of ice-cream."

"Two hundred? Yes—I suppose she had, with all the

Philadelphia connection coming." Delia pondered. "How about the doylies?" she inquired.

"With your aunt Cecilia Vandergrave's we shall manage beautifully."

"Yes. . . . Thank you, Charlotte, for taking all this trouble."

"Oh—" Charlotte protested, with her flitting sneer; and Delia perceived the irony of thanking a mother for occupying herself with the details of her own daughter's wedding.

"Do sit down, Chatty," she murmured, feeling herself redden at her blunder.

Charlotte, with a sigh, sat down on the nearest chair.

"We shall have a beautiful day tomorrow," she said, pensively surveying the placid heaven.

"Yes. Where is Tina?"

"She was very tired. I've sent her upstairs to lie down."

This seemed so eminently suitable that Delia made no immediate answer. After an interval she said: "We shall miss her."

Charlotte's reply was an inarticulate murmur.

The two cousins remained silent, Charlotte as usual bolt upright, her thin hands clutched on the arms of her old-fashioned rush-bottomed seat, Delia somewhat heavily sunk into the depths of a high-backed armchair. The two had exchanged their last remarks on the preparations for the morrow, and nothing more remained to be said as to the number of guests, the brewing of the punch, the arrangements for the robing of the clergy, and the disposal of the presents in the best spare-room.

Only one subject had not yet been touched on, and Delia, as she watched her cousin's profile grimly cut upon the melting twilight, waited for Charlotte to speak. But Charlotte remained silent.

"I have been thinking," Delia at length began, a slight tremor in her voice, "that I ought presently—"

She fancied she saw Charlotte's hands tighten on the knobs of the chair-arms.

"You ought presently—?"

"Well, before Tina goes to bed, perhaps go up for a few minutes—"

Charlotte remained silent, visibly resolved on making no effort to assist her.

"Tomorrow," Delia continued, "we shall be in such a rush from the earliest moment that I don't see how, in the midst of all the interruptions and excitement, I can possibly—"

"Possibly?" Charlotte monotonously echoed.

Delia felt her blush deepening through the dusk. "Well, I suppose you agree with me that a word ought to be said to the child as to the new duties and responsibilities that— well—what is usual, in fact, at such a time," she falteringly ended.

"Yes, I have thought of that," Charlotte answered abruptly. She said no more, but Delia divined in her the

stirring of that obscure opposition which, in the crucial moments of Tina's life, seemed automatically to manifest itself.
She could not understand why Charlotte should at times
grow so enigmatic and inaccessible, but she saw no reason
why this change of mood should interfere with what she
deemed to be her own duty. Tina must long for her guid-
ing hand into the new life as much as she yearned for the
exchanges of half-confidences which would be her real farewell to her adopted daughter. Her heart beating a little more
quickly than usual, she rose and walked through the open
window into the shadowy drawing-room. The moon, between the columns of the veranda, sent a broad light across
the rows of chairs, irradiated the lace-decked altar with its
empty candlesticks and vases, and outlined with silver Delia's
heavy reflection in the pier-glass.

She crossed the room toward the hall.

"Delia!" Charlotte's voice sounded behind her. She
turned, and the two women faced each other in the revealing light. Charlotte's face looked as it had looked on the
dreadful day when Delia had suddenly seen it in the glass
above her shoulder.

"You were going up now—to speak to Tina?" Charlotte asked.

"I—yes. It's nearly nine. I thought—"

"Yes; I understand." Miss Lovell made a visible effort
at self-control. "Please understand me too, Delia, if I ask
you—not to."

"Not to?" Delia scrutinized her cousin with a vague sense of apprehension. What mystery did this strange request conceal? But no—such a doubt as flitted across her mind was inadmissible. She was too sure of her Tina!

"I confess I don't understand you, Charlotte. You surely feel that, on the night before her wedding, a girl ought to have a mother's counsel, a mother's—"

"Yes: I feel that." Charlotte Lovell took a hurried breath. "But the question is: which of us is her mother?"

Delia drew back involuntarily. "Which of us?" she stammered.

"Yes. Oh, don't imagine it's the first time I've asked myself the question! There—I mean to be calm, quite calm. I don't intend to go back to the past. I've accepted—accepted everything—gratefully. Only tonight—just tonight."

Delia felt the rush of pity that always prevailed over every other feeling in her rare interchanges of truth with Charlotte Lovell. Her throat filled with tears, and she remained silent.

"Just tonight," Charlotte concluded, "*I'm* her mother."

"Charlotte! You're not going to tell her so—not now?" broke involuntarily from Delia.

Charlotte gave a faint laugh. "If I did, should you hate it as much as all that?"

"Hate it? What a word, between us!"

"Between us? But it's been between us since the beginning—the very beginning! Since the day when you discovered that Clement Spender hadn't quite broken his heart because he wasn't good enough for you, since you found your revenge and your triumph in keeping me at your mercy and in taking his child from me!" Charlotte's words flamed up as if from the depth of the infernal fires; then the blaze dropped, her head sank forward, and she stood before Delia dumb and stricken.

Delia's first movement was one of an indignant recoil. Where she had felt only tenderness, compassion, the impulse to help and befriend, these darknesses had been smoldering in the other's breast! It was as if a poisonous smoke had swept over some pure summer landscape.

Usually such feelings were quickly followed by a reaction of sympathy. But now she felt none. An utter weariness possessed her.

"Yes," she said slowly, "I sometimes believe you really have hated me from the very first, hated me for everything I've tried to do for you."

Charlotte raised her head sharply. "To do for me? But everything you've done has been done for Clement Spender!"

Delia stared at her with a kind of terror. "You are horrible, Charlotte. Upon my honor, I haven't thought of Clement Spender for years."

"Ah, but you have—you have! You've always thought of him in thinking of Tina—of him and nobody else! A woman never stops thinking of the man she loves. She thinks of him years afterward, in all sorts of unconscious ways, in thinking of all sorts of things—books, pictures, sunsets, a flower, or a ribbon—or a clock on the mantelpiece." Charlotte broke off with her sneering laugh. "That was what I gambled on, you see—that's why I came to you that day. I knew I was giving Tina another mother."

Again the poisonous smoke seemed to envelop Delia: that she and Charlotte, two spent old women, should be standing before Tina's bridal altar and talking to each other of hatred, seemed unimaginably hideous and degrading.

"You wicked woman—you *are* wicked!" she exclaimed.

Then the evil mist cleared away, and through it she saw the baffled, pitiful figure of the mother who was not a mother, and who, for every benefit accepted, felt herself robbed of a privilege. She moved nearer to Charlotte and laid a hand on her arm.

"Not here! Don't let us talk like this here."

The other drew away from her. "Wherever you please, then. I'm not particular!"

"But tonight, Charlotte—the night before Tina's wedding? Isn't every place in this house full of her? How could we go on saying cruel things to each other anywhere?" Charlotte was silent, and Delia continued in a steadier voice: "Nothing you say can really hurt me—for long; and I don't want to hurt you—I never did."

"You tell me that—and you've left nothing undone to divide me from my daughter! Do you suppose it's been easy, all these years, to hear her call you mother? Oh, I know, I know—it was agreed that she must never guess. But if you hadn't perpetually come between us, she'd have had no one but me, she'd have felt about me as a child feels about its mother, she'd have had to love me better than anyone else. With all your forbearances and your generosities, you've ended by robbing me of my child. And I've put up with it all for her sake—because I knew I had to. But tonight—tonight she belongs to me. Tonight I can't bear that she should call you mother."

Delia Ralston made no immediate reply. It seemed to her that for the first time she had sounded the deepest depths of maternal passion, and she stood awed at the echoes it gave back.

"How you must love her—to say such things to me!" she murmured; and then, with a final effort: "Yes, you're right. I won't go up to her. It's you who must go."

Charlotte started toward her impulsively; but with a hand lifted as if in defense, Delia moved across the room and out again to the veranda. As she sank down in her chair, she heard the drawing-room door open and close, and the sound of Charlotte's feet on the stairs.

Delia sat alone in the night. The last drop of her magnanimity had been spent, and she tried to avert her shuddering mind from Charlotte. What was happening at this moment upstairs? With what dark revelations were Tina's bridal dreams to be defaced? Well, that was not matter for conjecture, either. She, Delia Ralston, had played her part, done her utmost: there remained nothing now but to try to lift her spirit above the embittering sense of failure.

There was a strange element of truth in some of the things that Charlotte had said. With what divination that maternal passion had endowed her! Her jealousy seemed to have a million feelers. Yes; it was true that the sweetness and peace of Tina's bridal eve had been filled, for Delia, with visions of her own unrealized past. Softly, imperceptibly, it had reconciled her to the memory of what she had missed. All these last days she had been living the girl's life, she had been Tina, and Tina had been her own girlish self, the far-off Delia Lovell. Now for the first time, without shame, without self-reproach, without a pang or a scruple, Delia could yield to that vision of requited love from which her imagination had always turned away. She had made her choice in youth, and she had accepted it in maturity; and here in this bridal joy, so mysteriously her own, was the compensation for all she had missed and yet never renounced.

Delia understood now that Charlotte had guessed all this, and that the knowledge had filled her with a fierce resentment. Charlotte had said long ago that Clement Spender had never really belonged to her; now she had perceived that it was the same with Clement Spender's child. As the truth stole upon Delia, her heart melted with the old compassion for Charlotte. She saw that it was a terrible, a sacrilegious thing, to interfere with another's destiny, to lay the tenderest touch upon any human being's right to love and suffer after his own fashion. Delia had twice intervened in Charlotte Lovell's life: it was natural that Charlotte should be her enemy. If only she did not revenge herself by wounding Tina!

The adopted mother's thoughts reverted painfully to the little white room upstairs. She had meant her half-hour with Tina to leave the girl with thoughts as fragrant as the flowers she was to find beside her when she woke. And now—

Delia started up from her musing. There was a step on the stair—Charlotte coming down through the silent house. Delia stood up with a vague impulse of escape: she felt that she could not face her cousin's eyes. She turned the corner of the veranda, hoping to find the shutters of the dining-room unlatched, and to slip away unnoticed to her room; but in a moment Charlotte was beside her.

"Delia!"

"Ah, it's you? I was going up to bed." For the life of her Delia could not keep an edge of hardness from her voice.

"Yes: it's late. You must be very tired." Charlotte paused: her own voice was strained and painful.

"I *am* tired," Delia acknowledged.

In the moonlit hush the other went up to her, laying a timid touch on her arm.

"Not till you've seen Tina."

Delia stiffened. "Tina? But it's late! Isn't she sleeping? I thought you'd stay with her until—"

"I don't know if she's sleeping." Charlotte paused. "I haven't been in—but there's a light under her door."

"You haven't been in?"

"No: I just stood in the passage, and tried—"

"Tried—?"

"To think of something—something to say to her without—without her guessing." A sob stopped her, but she pressed on with a final effort. "It's no use. You were right: there's nothing I can say. You're her real mother. Go to her. It's not your fault—or mine."

"Oh—" Delia cried.

Charlotte clung to her in inarticulate abasement. "You said I was wicked—I'm not wicked. After all, she was mine when she was little!"

Delia put an arm about her shoulder.

"Hush, dear! We'll go to her together."

The other yielded automatically to her touch, and side by side the two women mounted the stairs, Charlotte timing her impetuous step to Delia's stiffened movements. They walked down the passage to Tina's door; but there Charlotte Lovell paused and shook her head.

"No—you," she whispered suddenly, and turned away.

Tina lay in bed, her arms folded under her head, her happy eyes reflecting the silver space of sky that filled the window. She smiled at Delia through her dream.

"I knew you'd come."

Delia sat down beside her, and their clasped hands lay upon the coverlet. They did not say much, after all; or else their communion had no need of words. Delia never knew how long she sat by the child's side: she abandoned herself to the spell of the moonlit hour.

But suddenly she thought of Charlotte, alone behind the shut door of her own room, watching, struggling, listening. Delia must not, for her own pleasure, prolong that tragic vigil. She bent down to kiss Tina goodnight; then she paused on the threshold and turned back.

"Darling! Just one thing more."

"Yes?" Tina murmured.

"I want you to promise me—"

"Everything, everything, you darling!"

"Well, then, that when you go away tomorrow—at the very last moment, you understand—"

"Yes?"

"After you've said good-by to me, and to everybody else—just as Lanning helps you into the carriage—"

"Yes?"

"That you'll give your last kiss to Aunt Charlotte. Don't forget—the very last."

HENRY JAMES

THE REAL THING

—

CHAPTER I

When the porter's wife (she used to answer the house-bell),
announced "A gentleman—with a lady, sir," I had, as I often
had in those days, for the wish was father to the thought—
an immediate vision of sitters. Sitters my visitors in this
case proved to be; but not in the sense I should have preferred. However, there was nothing at first to indicate that
they might not have come for a portrait. The gentleman, a
man of fifty, very high and very straight, with a moustache
slightly grizzled and a dark gray walking-coat admirably fit-
ted, both of which I noted professionally—I don't mean
as a barber or yet as a tailor—would have struck me as a
celebrity if celebrities often were striking. It was a truth of
which I had for some time been conscious that a figure with
a good deal of frontage was, as one might say, almost never
a public institution. A glance at the lady helped to remind
me of this paradoxical law: she also looked too distinguished

to be a "personality." Moreover one would scarcely come across two variations together.

Neither of the pair spoke immediately—they only prolonged the preliminary gaze which suggested that each wished to give the other a chance. They were visibly shy; they stood there letting me take them in—which, as I afterwards perceived, was the most practical thing they could have done. In this way their embarrassment served their cause. I had seen people painfully reluctant to mention that they desired anything so gross as to be represented on canvas; but the scruples of my new friends appeared almost insurmountable. Yet the gentleman might have said "I should like a portrait of my wife," and the lady might have said "I should like a portrait of my husband." Perhaps they were not husband and wife—this naturally would make the matter more delicate. Perhaps they wished to be done together—in which case they ought to have brought a third person to break the news.

"We come from Mr. Rivet," the lady said at last, with a dim smile which had the effect of a moist sponge passed over a "sunk" piece of painting, as well as of a vague allusion to vanished beauty. She was as tall and straight, in her degree, as her companion, and with ten years less to carry. She looked as sad as a woman could look whose face was not charged with expression; that is her tinted oval mask showed friction as an exposed surface shows it. The hand of time had played over her freely, but only to simplify. She was slim and stiff, and so well-dressed, in dark blue cloth, with lappets and pockets and buttons, that it was clear she employed the same tailor as her husband. The couple had an indefinable air of prosperous thrift—they evidently got a good deal of luxury for their money. If I was to be one of their luxuries it would behove me to consider my terms.

"Ah, Claude Rivet recommended me?" I inquired; and I added that it was very kind of him, though I could reflect that, as he only painted landscape, this was not a sacrifice.

The lady looked very hard at the gentleman, and the gentleman looked round the room. Then staring at the floor a moment and stroking his moustache, he rested his pleasant eyes on me with the remark: "He said you were the right one."

"I try to be, when people want to sit."

"Yes, we should like to," said the lady anxiously.

"Do you mean together?"

My visitors exchanged a glance. "If you could do anything with *me* I suppose it would be double," the gentleman stammered.

"Oh yes, there's naturally a higher charge for two figures than for one."

"We should like to make it pay," the husband confessed.

"That's very good of you," I returned, appreciating so unwonted a sympathy—for I supposed he meant pay the artist.

A sense of strangeness seemed to dawn on the lady. "We mean for the illustrations—Mr. Rivet said you might put one in."

"Put one in—an illustration?" I was equally confused.

"Sketch her off, you know," said the gentleman, coloring.

It was only then that I understood the service Claude Rivet had rendered me; he had told them that I worked in black and white, for magazines, for story-books, for sketches of contemporary life, and consequently had fequent employment for models. These things were true, but it was not less true (I may confess it now—whether because the aspiration was to lead to everything or to nothing I leave the reader to guess), that I couldn't get the honors, to say nothing of the emoluments, of a great painter of portraits out of my head. My "illustrations" were my pot-boilers; I looked to a different branch of art (far and away the most interesting it had always seemed to me), to perpetuate my fame. There was no shame in looking to it also to make my fortune; but that fortune was by so much further from being made from the moment my visitors wished to be "done" for nothing. I was disappointed; for in the pictorial sense I had immediately *seen* them. I had seized their type—I had already settled what I would do with it. Something that wouldn't absolutely have pleased them, I afterwards reflected.

"Ah you're—you're—a—?" I began, as soon as I had mastered my surprise. I couldn't bring out the dingy word "models"; it seemed to fit the case so little.

"We haven't had much practice," said the lady.

"We've got to *do* something, and we've thought that an

artist in your line might perhaps make something of us," her husband threw off. He further mentioned that they didn't know many artists and that they had gone first, on the off-chance (he painted views of course, but sometimes put in figures—perhaps I remembered), to Mr. Rivet, whom they had met a few years before at a place in Norfolk where he was sketching.

"We used to sketch a little ourselves," the lady hinted.

"It's very awkward, but we absolutely *must* do something," her husband went on.

"Of course we're not so *very* young," she admitted, with a wan smile.

With the remark that I might as well know something more about them, the husband had handed me a card extracted from a neat new pocket-book (their appurtenances were all of the freshest) and inscribed with the words "Major Monarch." Impressive as these words were they didn't carry my knowledge much further; but my visitor presently added: "I've left the army, and we've had the misfortune to lose our money. In fact our means are dreadfully small."

"It's an awful bore," said Mrs. Monarch.

They evidently wished to be discreet—to take care not to swagger because they were gentlefolks. I perceived they would have been willing to recognize this as something of a drawback, at the same time that I guessed at an underlying sense—their consolation in adversity—that they *had* their points. They certainly had; but these advantages struck me as preponderantly social; such for instance as would help to make a drawing-room look well. However, a drawing-room was always, or ought to be, a picture.

In consequence of his wife's allusion to their age Major Monarch observed: "Naturally, it's more for the figure that we thought of going in. We can still hold ourselves up." On the instant I saw that the figure was indeed their strong point. His "naturally" didn't sound vain, but it lighted up the question. "*She* has got the best," he continued, nodding at his wife, with a pleasant after-dinner absence of circumlocution. I could only reply, as if we were in fact sitting over our wine, that this didn't prevent his own from being very good; which led him in turn to rejoin: "We thought that if you ever have to do people like us, we might be something like it. *She*, particularly—for a lady in a book, you know."

I was so amused by them that, to get more of it, I did my best to take their point of view; and though it was an embarrassment to find myself appraising physically, as if they were animals on hire or useful blacks, a pair whom I should have expected to meet only in one of the relations in which criticism is tacit, I looked at Mrs. Monarch judicially enough to be able to exclaim, after a moment, with conviction: "Oh yes, a lady in a book!" She was singularly like a bad illustration.

"We'll stand up, if you like," said the Major; and he raised himself before me with a really grand air.

I could take his measure at a glance—he was six feet two and a perfect gentleman. It would have paid any club in process of formation and in want of a stamp to engage him at a salary to stand in the principal window. What struck me immediately was that in coming to me they had rather missed their vocation; they could surely have been turned to better account for advertising purposes. I couldn't of course see the thing in detail, but I could see them make somebody's fortune—I don't mean their own. There was something in them for a waistcoat-maker, an hotel-keeper, or a soap-vendor. I could imagine "We always use it" pinned on their bosoms with the greatest effect; I had a vision of the promptitude with which they would launch a table d'hôte.

Mrs. Monarch sat still, not from pride but from shyness, and presently her husband said to her: "Get up my dear and show how smart you are." She obeyed, but she had no need to get up to show it. She walked to the end of the studio, and then she came back blushing, with her fluttered eyes on her husband. I was reminded of an incident I had accidentally had a glimpse of in Paris—being with a friend there, a dramatist about to produce a play—when an actress came to him to ask to be entrusted with a part. She went through her paces before him, walked up and down as Mrs. Monarch was doing. Mrs. Monarch did it quite as well, but I abstained from applauding. It was very odd to see such people apply for such poor pay. She looked as if she had ten thousand a year. Her husband had used the word that described her: she was, in the London current jargon, essentially and typically "smart." Her figure was, in the same order of ideas, conspicuously and irreproachably "good." For a woman of her age her waist was surprisingly small; her elbow moreover had the orthodox crook. She held her head at the conventional angle; but why did she come to *me*? She ought to have tried on jackets at a big shop. I feared my visitors were not only destitute, but "artistic"—which would be a great complication. When she sat down again I thanked her, observing that what a draughtsman most valued in his model was the faculty of keeping quiet.

"Oh, *she* can keep quiet," said Major Monarch. Then he added, jocosely: "I've always kept her quiet."

"I'm not a nasty fidget, am I?" Mrs. Monarch appealed to her husband.

He addressed his answer to me. "Perhaps it isn't out of place to mention—because we ought to be quite business-like, oughtn't we?—that when I married her she was known as the Beautiful Statue."

"Oh dear!" said Mrs. Monarch, ruefully.

"Of course I should want a certain amount of expression," I rejoined.

"Of *course*!" they both exclaimed.

"And then I suppose you know that you'll get awfully tired."

"Oh, we *never* get tired!" they eagerly cried.

"Have you had any kind of practice?"

They hesitated—they looked at each other. We've been photographed, *immensely*," said Mrs. Monarch.

"She means the fellows have asked us," added the Major.

"I see—because you're so good-looking."

"I don't know what they thought, but they were always after us."

"We always got our photographs for nothing," smiled Mrs. Monarch.

"We might have brought some, my dear," her husband remarked.

"I'm not sure we have any left. We've given quantities away," she explained to me.

"With our autographs and that sort of thing," said the Major.

"Are they to be got in the shops?" I inquired as a harmless pleasantry.

"Oh yes, *hers*—they used to be."

"Not now," said Mrs. Monarch, with her eyes on the floor.

CHAPTER II

I could fancy the "sort of thing" they put on the presentation copies of their photographs, and I was sure they wrote a beautiful hand. It was odd how quickly I was sure of everything that concerned them. If they were now so poor as to have to earn shillings and pence, they never had had much of a margin. Their good looks had been their capital, and they had good-humoredly made the most of the career that this resource marked out for them. It was in their faces, the blankness, the deep intellectual repose of the twenty years of country-house visiting which had given them pleasant intonations. I could see the sunny drawing-rooms, sprinkled with periodicals she didn't read, in which Mrs. Monarch had continuously sat; I could see the wet shrubberies in which she had walked, equipped to admiration for either exercise. I could see the rich covers the Major had helped to shoot and the wonderful garments in which, late at night, he repaired to the smoking-room to talk about them. I could imagine their leggings and waterproofs, their knowing tweeds and rugs, their rolls of sticks and cases of tackle and neat umbrellas; and I could evoke the exact appearance of their servants and the compact variety of their luggage on the platforms of country stations.

They gave small tips, but they were liked; they didn't do anything themselves, but they were welcome. They looked so well everywhere; they gratified the general relish for stature, complexion, and "form." They knew it without fatuity or vulgarity, and they respected themselves in consequence. They were not superficial: they were thorough and kept themselves up—it had been their line. People with such a taste for activity had to have some line. I could feel how, even in a dull house, they could have been counted upon for cheerfulness. At present something had happened—it didn't matter what, their little income had grown less, it had grown least—and they had to do something for pocket-money. Their friends liked them, but didn't like to support them. There was something about them that represented credit—their clothes, their manners, their type; but if credit is a large empty pocket in which an occasional chink reverberates, the chink at least must be audible. What they wanted of me was help to make it so. Fortunately they had no children—I soon divined that. They would also perhaps wish our relations to be kept secret: this was why it was "for the figure"—the reproduction of the face would betray them.

I liked them—they were so simple; and I had no objection to them if they would suit. But, somehow, with all their perfections I didn't easily believe in them. After all they were amateurs, and the ruling passion of my life was the detestation of the amateur. Combined with this was another perversity—an innate preference for the represented subject over the real one: the defect of the real one was so apt to be a lack of representation. I liked things that appeared; then one was sure. Whether they *were* or not was a subordinate and almost always a profitless question. There were other considerations, the first of which was that I already had two or three people in use, notably a young person with big feet, in alpaca, from Kilburn, who for a couple of years had come to me regularly for my illustrations and with whom I was still—perhaps ignobly—satisfied. I frankly explained to my visitors how the case stood; but they had taken more precautions than I supposed. They had reasoned out their opportunity, for Claude Rivet had told them of the projected *édition de luxe* of one of the writers of our day—the rarest of the novelists—who, long neglected by the multitudinous vulgar and dearly prized by the attentive (need I mention Philip

Vincent?) had had the happy fortune of seeing, late in life, the dawn and then the full light of a higher criticism—an estimate in which, on the part of the public, there was something really of expiation. The edition in question, planned by a publisher of taste, was practically an act of high reparation; the wood-cuts with which it was to be enriched were the homage of English art to one of the most independent representatives of English letters. Major and Mrs. Monarch confessed to me that they had hoped I might be able to work *them* into my share of the enterprise. They knew I was to do the first of the books, "Rutland Ramsay," but I had to make clear to them that my participation in the rest of the affair—this first book was to be a test—was to depend on the satisfaction I should give. If this should be limited my employers would drop me without a scruple. It was therefore a crisis for me, and naturally I was making special preparations, looking about for new people, if they should be necessary, and securing the best types. I admitted however that I should like to settle down to two or three good models who would do for everything.

"Should we have often to—a—put on special clothes?" Mrs. Monarch timidly demanded.

"Dear, yes—that's half the business."

"And should we be expected to supply our own costumes?"

"Oh, no ; I've got a lot of things. A painter's models put on—or put off—anything he likes."

"And do you mean—a—the same?"

"The same?"

Mrs. Monarch looked at her husband again.

"Oh, she was just wondering," he explained, "if the costumes are in *general* use." I had to confess that they were, and I mentioned further that some of them (I had a lot of genuine, greasy last-century things), had served their time, a hundred years ago, on living, world-stained men and women. "We'll put on anything that *fits*," said the Major.

"Oh, I arrange that—they fit in the pictures."

"I'm afraid I should do better for the modern books. I would come as you like," said Mrs. Monarch.

"She has got a lot of clothes at home: they might do for contemporary life," her husband continued.

"Oh, I can fancy scenes in which you'd be quite natural." And indeed I could see the slipshod rearrangements of stale properties—the stories I tried to produce pictures for without the exasperation of reading them—whose sandy tracts the good lady might help to people. But I had to return to the fact that for this sort of work—the daily mechanical grind—I was already equipped: the people I was working with were fully adequate.

"We only thought we might be more like *some* characters," said Mrs. Monarch mildly, getting up.

Her husband also rose; he stood looking at me with a dim wistfulness that was touching in so fine a man. "Wouldn't it be rather a pull sometimes to have—a—to have—?" He hung fire; he wanted me to help him by phrasing what he meant. But I couldn't—I didn't know. So he brought it out awkwardly: "The *real* thing; a gentleman, you know, or a lady." I was quite ready to give a general assent—I admitted that there was a great deal in that. This encouraged Major Monarch to say, following up his appeal with an unacted gulp: "It's awfully hard—we've tried everything." The gulp was communicative; it proved too much for his wife. Before I knew it Mrs. Monarch had dropped again upon a divan and burst into tears. Her husband sat down beside her, holding one of her hands; whereupon she quickly dried her eyes with the other, while I felt embarrassed as she looked up at me. "There isn't a confounded job I haven't applied for—waited for—prayed for. You can fancy we'd be pretty bad first. Secretaryships and that sort of thing? You might as well ask for a peerage. I'd be *anything*—I'm strong; a messenger or a coalheaver. I'd put on a gold-laced cap and open carriage-doors in front of the haberdasher's; I'd hang about a station to carry portmanteaus; I'd be a postman. But they won't *look* at you; there are thousands, as good as yourself, already on the ground. *Gentlemen*, poor beggars, who have drunk their wine, who have kept their hunters!"

I was as reassuring as I knew how to be, and my visitors were presently on their feet again while, for the experiment, we agreed on an hour. We were discussing it when the door opened and Miss Churm came in with a wet umbrella. Miss Churm had to take the omnibus to Maida Vale and then walk half-a-mile. She looked a trifle blowsy and slightly splashed. I scarcely ever saw her come in without thinking afresh how odd it was that, being so little in herself, she should yet be so much in others. She was a meager little Miss Churm, but she was an ample heroine of romance. She was only a freckled cockney, but she could represent everything, from a fine lady to a shepherdess; she had the faculty, as she might have had a fine voice or long hair. She couldn't spell, and she loved beer, but she had two or three "points," and practice, and a knack, and mother-wit, and a kind of whimsical sensibility, and a love of the theater, and seven sisters, and not an ounce of respect, especially for the *h*. The first thing my visitors saw was that her umbrella was wet, and in their spotless perfection they visibly winced at it. The rain had come on since their arrival.

"I'm all in a soak; there *was* a mess of people in the 'bus. I wish you lived near a stytion," said Miss Churm. I requested her to get ready as quickly as possible, and she passed into the room in which she always changed her dress. But before going out she asked me what she was to get into this time.

"It's the Russian princess, don't you know?" I answered; "the one with the 'golden eyes,' in black velvet, for the long thing in the *Cheapside*."

"Golden eyes? I *say*!" cried Miss Churm, while my companions watched her with intensity as she withdrew. She always arranged herself, when she was late, before I could turn round; and I kept my visitors a little, on purpose, so that they might get an idea, from seeing her, what would be expected of themselves. I mentioned that she was quite my notion of an excellent model—she was really very clever.

"Do you think she looks like a Russian princess?" Major Monarch asked, with lurking alarm.

"When I make her, yes."

"Oh, if you have to *make* her—!" he reasoned, acutely.

"That's the most you can ask. There are so many that are not makeable."

"Well now, *here's* a lady"—and with a persuasive smile he passed his arm into his wife's—"who's already made!"

"Oh, I'm not a Russian princess," Mrs. Monarch protested, a little coldly. I could see that she had known some and didn't like them. There, immediately, was a complication of a kind that I never had to fear with Miss Churm.

This young lady came back in black velvet—the gown was rather rusty and very low on her lean shoulders—and with a Japanese fan in her red hands. I reminded her that in the scene I was doing she had to look over someone's head. "I forget whose it is; but it doesn't matter. Just look over a head."

"I'd rather look over a stove," said Miss Churm; and she took her station near the fire. She fell into position, settled herself into a tall attitude, gave a certain backward inclination to her head and a certain forward droop to her fan, and looked, at least to my prejudiced sense, distinguished and charming, foreign and dangerous. We left her looking so, while I went down-stairs with Major and Mrs. Monarch.

"I think I could come about as near it as that," said Mrs. Monarch.

"Oh, you think she's shabby, but you must allow for the alchemy of art."

However, they went off with an evident increase of comfort, founded on their demonstrable advantage in being the real thing. I could fancy them shuddering over Miss Churm. She was very droll about them when I went back, for I told her what they wanted.

"Well, if *she* can sit I'll tyke to bookkeeping," said my model.

"She's very lady-like," I replied, as an innocent form of aggravation.

"So much the worse for *you*. That means she can't turn round."

"She'll do for the fashionable novels."

"Oh yes, she'll *do* for them!" my model humorously declared. "Ain't they bad enough without her?" I had often sociably denounced them to Miss Churm.

CHAPTER III

It was for the elucidation of a mystery in one of these works that I first tried Mrs. Monarch. Her husband came with her, to be useful if necessary—it was sufficiently clear that as a general thing he would prefer to come with her. At first I wondered if this were for "propriety's" sake—if he were going to be jealous and meddling. The idea was too tiresome, and if it had been confirmed it would speedily have brought our acquaintance to a close. But I soon saw there was nothing in it and that if he accompanied Mrs. Monarch it was (in addition to the chance of being wanted), simply because he had nothing else to do. When she was away from him his occupation was gone—she never *had* been away from him. I judged, rightly, that in their awkward situation their close union was their main comfort and that this union had no weak spot. It was a real marriage, an encouragement to the hesitating, a nut for pessimists to crack. Their address was humble (I remember afterwards thinking it had been the only thing about them that was really professional), and I could fancy the lamentable lodgings in which the Major would have been left alone. He could bear them with his wife—he couldn't bear them without her.

He had too much tact to try and make himself agreeable when he couldn't be useful; so he simply sat and waited, when I was too absorbed in my work to talk. But I liked to make him talk—it made my work, when it didn't interrupt it, less sordid, less special. To listen to him was to combine the excitement of going out with the economy of staying at home. There was only one hindrance: that I seemed not to know any of the people he and his wife had known. I think he wondered extremely, during the term of our intercourse, whom the deuce I *did* know. He hadn't a stray sixpence of an idea to fumble for; so we didn't spin it very fine— we confined ourselves to questions of leather and even of liquor (saddlers and breeches-makers and how to get good claret cheap), and matters like "good trains" and the habits of small game. His lore on these last subjects was astonishing, he managed to interweave the station-master with the ornithologist. When he couldn't talk about greater things he could talk cheerfully about smaller, and since I couldn't accompany him into reminiscences of the fashionable world he could lower the conversation without a visible effort to my level.

So earnest a desire to please was touching in a man who could so easily have knocked one down. He looked after the fire and had an opinion on the draught of the stove, without my asking him, and I could see that he thought many of my arrangements not half clever enough. I remember telling him that if I were only rich I would offer him a salary to come and teach me how to live. Sometimes he gave a random sigh, of which the essence was: "Give me even such a bare old barrack as *this*, and I'd do something with it!" When I wanted to use him he came alone; which was an illustration of the superior courage of women. His wife could bear her solitary second floor, and she was in general more discreet; showing by various small reserves that she was alive to the propriety of keeping our relations markedly professional—not letting them slide into sociability. She wished it to remain clear that she and the Major were employed, not cultivated, and if she approved of me as a superior, who could be kept in his place, she never thought me quite good enough for an equal.

She sat with great intensity, giving the whole of her mind to it, and was capable of remaining for an hour almost as motionless as if she were before a photographer's lens. I could see she had been photographed often, but somehow the very habit that made her good for that purpose unfitted her for mine. At first I was extremely pleased with her lady-like air, and it was a satisfaction, on coming to follow her lines, to see how good they were and how far they could lead the pencil. But after a few times I began to find her too insurmountably stiff; do what I would with it my drawing looked like a photograph or a copy of a photograph. Her figure had no variety of expression—she herself had no sense of variety. You may say that this was my business, was only a question of placing her. I placed her in every conceivable position, but she managed to obliterate their differences. She was always a lady certainly, and into the bargain was always the same lady. She was the real thing, but always the same thing. There were moments when I was opressed by the serenity of her confidence that she *was* the real thing. All her dealings with me and all her husband's were an implication that this was lucky for *me*. Meanwhile I found myself trying to invent types that approached her own, instead of making her own transform itself—in the clever way that was not impossible, for instance, to poor Miss Churm. Arrange as I would and take the precautions I would, she always, in my pictures, came out too tall—landing me in the dilemma of having represented a fascinating woman as seven feet high, which, out of respect perhaps to my own very much scantier inches, was far from my idea of such a personage.

The case was worse with the Major—nothing I could do would keep *him* down, so that he became useful only for the representation of brawny giants. I adored variety and range, I cherished human accidents, the illustrative note; I wanted to characterize closely, and the thing in the world I most hated was the danger of being ridden by a type. I had quarreled with some of my friends about it—I had parted company with them for maintaining that one *had* to be, and that if the type was beautiful (witness Raphael and Leonardo) the servitude was only a gain. I was neither Leonardo nor Raphael; I might only be a presumptuous young modern searcher, but I held that everything was to be sacrificed sooner than character. When they averred that the haunty type in question could easily *be* character, I retorted, perhaps superficially: "Whose?" It couldn't be everybody's—it might end in being nobody's.

After I had drawn Mrs. Monarch a dozen times I perceived more clearly than before that the value of such a model as Miss Churm resided precisely in the fact that she had no positive stamp, combined of course with the other fact that what she did have was a curious and inexplicable talent for imitation. Her usual appearance was like a curtain which she could draw up at request for a capital performance. This performance was simply suggestive; but it was a word to the wise—it was vivid and pretty. Sometimes, even, I thought it, though she was plain herself, too insipidly pretty; I made it a reproach to her that the figures drawn from her were monotonously (*bêtement*, as we used to say) graceful. Nothing made her more angry: it was so much her pride to feel that she could sit for characters that had nothing in common with each other. She would accuse me at such moments of taking away her "reputytion."

It suffered a certain shrinkage, this queer quantity, from the repeated visits of my new friends. Miss Churm was greatly in demand, never in want of employment, so I had no scruple in putting her off occasionally, to try them more at my ease. It was certainly amusing at first to do the real thing—it was amusing to do Major Monarch's trousers. They *were* the real thing, even if he did come out colossal. It was amusing to do his wife's back hair (it was so mathematically neat) and the particular "smart" tension of her tight stays. She lent herself especially to positions in which the face was somewhat averted or blurred; she abounded in lady-like back views and *profils perdus*. When she stood erect she took naturally one of the attitudes in which court-painters represent queens and princesses; so that I found myself wondering whether, to draw out this accomplishment, I couldn't get the editor of the *Cheapside* to publish a really royal romance, "A Tale of Buckingham Palace." Sometimes, however, the real thing and the make-believe came into contact; by which I mean that Miss Churm, keeping an appointment or coming to make one on days when I had much work in hand, encountered her invidious rivals. The encounter was not on their part, for they noticed her no more than if she had been the housemaid; not from intentional loftiness, but simply because, as yet, professionally, they didn't know how to fraternize, as I could guess that they would have liked—or at least that the Major would. They couldn't talk about the omnibus—they always walked; and they didn't know what else to try—she wasn't interested in good trains or cheap claret. Besides, they must have felt—in the air—that she was amused at them, secretly derisive of their ever knowing how. She was not a person to conceal her skepticism if she had had a chance to show it. On the other hand Mrs. Monarch didn't think her tidy; for why else did she take pains to say to me (it was going out of the way, for Mrs. Monarch), that she didn't like dirty women?

One day when my young lady happened to be present with my other sitters (she even dropped in, when it was convenient, for a chat), I asked her to be so good as to lend a hand in getting tea—a service with which she was familiar and which was one of a class that, living as I did in a small way, with slender domestic resources, I often appealed to my models to render. They liked to lay hands on my property, to break the sitting, and sometimes the china—I made them feel Bohemian. The next time I saw Miss Churm after this incident she surprised me greatly by making a scene about it—she accused me of having wished to humiliate her. She had not resented the outrage at the time, but had seemed obliging and amused, enjoying the comedy of asking Mrs. Monarch, who sat vague and silent, whether she would have cream and sugar, and putting an exaggerated simper into the question. She had tried intonations—as if she too wished to pass for the real thing; till I was afraid my other visitors would take offense.

Oh, *they* were determined not to do this; and their touching patience was the measure of their great need. They would sit by the hour, uncomplaining, till I was ready to use them; they would come back on the chance of being wanted and would walk away cheerfully if they were not. I used to go to the door with them to see in what magnificent order they retreated. I tried to find other employment for them—I introduced them to several artists. But they didn't "take," for reasons I could appreciate, and I became conscious, rather anxiously, that after such disappointments they fell back upon me with a heavier weight. They did me the honor to think that it was I who was most *their* form. They were not picturesque enough for the painters, and in those days there were not so many serious workers in black and white. Besides, they had an eye to the great job I had mentioned to them—they had secretly set their hearts on supplying the right essence for my pictorial vindication of our fine novelist. They knew that for this undertaking I should want no costume-effects, none of the frippery of past ages—that it was a case in which everything would be contemporary and satirical and, presumably, genteel. If I could work them into it their future would be assured, for the labor would of course be long and the occupation steady.

One day Mrs. Monarch came without her husband—she explained his absence by his having had to go to the City. While she sat there in her usual anxious stiffness there came, at the door, a knock which I immediately recognized as the subdued appeal of a model out of work. It was followed by the entrance of a young man whom I at once perceived to be a foreigner and who proved in fact an Italian acquainted with no English word but my name, which he uttered in a way that made it seem to include all others. I had not then visited his country, nor was I proficient in his tongue; but as he was not so meanly constituted—what Italian is?—as to depend only on that member for expression he conveyed to me, in familiar but graceful mimicry, that he was in search of exactly the employment in which the lady before me was engaged. I was not struck with him at first, and while I continued to draw I emitted rough sounds of discouragement and dismissal. He stood his ground, however, not importunately, but with a dumb dog-like fidelity in his eyes which amounted to innocent impudence—the manner of a devoted servant (he might have been in the house for years), unjustly suspected. Suddenly I saw that this very attitude and expression made a picture, whereupon I told him to sit down and wait till I should be free. There was another picture in the way he obeyed me, and I observed as I worked that there were others still in the way he looked wonderingly, with his head thrown back, about the high studio. He might have been crossing himself in Saint Peter's. Before I finished I said to myself: "The fellow's a bankrupt orange-monger, but he's a treasure."

When Mrs. Monarch withdrew he passed across the room like a flash to open the door for her, standing there with the rapt, pure gaze of the young Dante spellbound by the young Beatrice. As I never insisted, in such situations, on the blankness of the British domestic, I reflected that he had the making of a servant (and I needed one, but couldn't pay him to be only that), as well as of a model; in short I made up my mind to adopt my bright adventurer if he would agree to officiate in the double capacity. He jumped at my offer, and in the event my rashness (for I had known nothing about him), was not brought home to me. He proved a sympathetic though a desultory ministrant, and had in a wonderful degree the *sentiment de la pose*. It was uncultivated, instinctive; a part of the happy instinct which had guided him to my door and helped him to spell out my name on the card nailed to it. He had had no other introduction to me than a guess, from the shape of my high north window, seen outside, that my place was a studio and that as a studio it would contain an artist. He had wandered to England in search of fortune, like other itinerants, and had embarked, with a partner and a small green handcart, on the sale of penny ices. The ices had melted away and the partner had dissolved in their train. My young man wore tight yellow trousers with reddish stripes and his name was Oronte. He was sallow but fair, and when I put him into some old clothes of my own he looked like an Englishman. He was as good as Miss Churm, who could look, when requested, like an Italian.

CHAPTER IV

I thought Mrs. Monarch's face slightly convulsed when, on her coming back with her husband, she found Oronte installed. It was strange to have to recognize in a scrap of a lazzarone a competitor to her magnificent Major. It was she who scented danger first, for the Major was anecdotically unconscious. But Oronte gave us tea, with a hundred eager confusions (he had never seen such a queer process), and I think she thought better of me for having at last an "establishment." They saw a couple of drawings that I had made of the establishment, and Mrs. Monarch hinted that it never would have struck her that he had sat for them. "Now the drawings you make from *us*, they look exactly like us," she reminded me, smiling in triumph; and I recognized that this was indeed just their defect. When I drew the Monarchs I couldn't, somehow, get away from them—get into the character I wanted to represent; and I had not the least desire my model should be discoverable in my picture. Miss Churm never was, and Mrs. Monarch thought I hid her, very properly, because she was vulgar; whereas if she was lost it was only as the dead who go to heaven are lost—in the gain of an angel the more.

By this time I had got a certain start with "Rutland Ramsay," the first novel in the great projected series; that is I had produced a dozen drawings, several with the help of the Major and his wife, and I had sent them in for approval. My understanding with the publishers, as I have already hinted, had been that I was to be left to do my work, in this particular case, as I liked, with the whole book committed to me; but my connection with the rest of the series was only contingent. There were moments when, frankly, it *was* a comfort to have the real thing under one's hand; for there were characters in "Rutland Ramsay" that were very much like it. There were people presumably as straight as the

Major and women of as good a fashion as Mrs. Monarch. There was a great deal of country-house life—treated, it is true, in a fine, fanciful, ironical, generalized way—and there was a considerable implication of knickerbockers and kilts. There were certain things I had to settle at the outset; such things for instance as the exact appearance of the hero, the particular bloom of the heroine. The author of course gave me a lead, but there was a margin for interpretation. I took the Monarchs into my confidence, I told them frankly what I was about, I mentioned my embarrassments and alternatives. "Oh, take *him*!" Mrs. Monarch murmured sweetly, looking at her husband; and "What could you want better than my wife?" the Major inquired, with the comfortable candor that now prevailed between us.

I was not obliged to answer these remarks—I was only obliged to place my sitters. I was not easy in mind, and I postponed, a little timidly perhaps, the solution of the question. The book was a large canvas, the other figures were numerous, and I worked off at first some of the episodes in which the hero and the heroine were not concerned. When once I had set *them* up I should have to stick to them—I couldn't make my young man seven feet high in one place and five feet nine in another. I inclined on the whole to the latter measurement, though the Major more than once reminded me that *he* looked about as young as anyone. It was indeed quite possible to arrange him, for the figure, so that it would have been difficult to detect his age. After the spontaneous Oronte had been with me a month, and after I had given him to understand several different times over that his native exuberance would presently constitute an insurmountable barrier to our further intercourse, I waked to a sense of his heroic capacity. He was only five feet seven, but the remaining inches were latent. I tried him almost secretly at first, for I was really rather afraid of the judgement my other models would pass on such a choice. If they regarded Miss Churm as little better than a snare, what would they think of the representation by a person so little the real thing as an Italian street-vendor of a protagonist formed by a public school?

If I went a little in fear of them it was not because they bullied me, because they had got an oppressive foothold, but because in their really pathetic decorum and mysteriously permanent newness they counted on me so intensely. I was therefore very glad when Jack Hawley came home: he was always of such good counsel. He painted badly himself, but there was no one like him for putting his finger on the place. He had been absent from England for a year; he had been somewhere—I don't remember where—to get a fresh eye. I was in a good deal of dread of any such organ, but we were old friends; he had been away for months and a sense of emptiness was creeping into my life. I hadn't dodged a missile for a year.

He came back with a fresh eye, but with the same old black velvet blouse, and the first evening he spent in my studio we smoked cigarettes till the small hours. He had done no work himself, he had only got the eye; so the field was clear for the production of my little things. He wanted to see what I had done for the *Cheapside*, but he was disappointed in the exhibition. That at least seemed the meaning of two or three comprehensive groans which, as he lounged on my big divan, on a folding leg, looking at my latest drawings, issued from his lips with the smoke of the cigarette.

"What's the matter with you?" I asked.

"What's the matter with *you*?"

"Nothing save that I'm mystified."

"You are indeed. You're quite off the hinge. What's the meaning of this new fad?" And he tossed me, with visible irreverence, a drawing in which I happened to have depicted both my majestic models. I asked if he didn't think it good, and he replied that it struck him as execrable, given the sort of thing I had always represented myself to him as wishing to arrive at; but I let that pass, I was so anxious to see exactly what he meant. The two figures in the picture looked colossal, but I supposed this was *not* what he meant, inasmuch as, for aught he knew to the contrary, I might have been trying for that. I maintained that I was working exactly in the same way as when he last had done me the honor to commend me. "Well, there's a big hole somewhere," he answered; "wait a bit and I'll discover it." I depended upon him to do so: where else was the fresh eye? But he produced at last nothing more luminous than "I don't know—I don't like your types." This was lame, for a critic who had never consented to discuss with me anything but the question of execution, the direction of strokes, and the mystery of values.

"In the drawings you've been looking at I think my types are very handsome."

"Oh, they won't do!"

"I've had a couple of new models."

"I see you have. *They* won't do."

"Are you very sure of that?"

"Absolutely—they're stupid."

"You mean *I* am—for I ought to get round that."

"You *can't*—with such people. Who are they?"

I told him, so far as was necessary, and he declared, heartlessly: "*Ce sont des gens qu'il faut mettre à la porte.*"

"You've never seen them; they're awfully good," I compassionately objected.

"Not seen them? Why, all this recent work of yours drops to pieces with them. It's all I want to see of them."

"No one else has said anything against it—the *Cheapside* people are pleased."

"Everyone else is an ass, and the *Cheapside* people the biggest asses of all. Come, don't pretend, at this time of day, to have pretty illusions about the public, especially about publishers and editors. It's not for *such* animals you work—it's for those who know, *coloro che sanno*; so keep straight for *me* if you can't keep straight for yourself. There's a certain sort of thing you tried for from the first—and a very good thing it is. But this twaddle isn't *in* it." When I talked with Hawley later about "Rutland Ramsay" and its possible successors he declared that I must get back into my boat again or I would go to the bottom. His voice in short was the voice of warning.

I noted the warning, but I didn't turn my friends out of doors. They bored me a good deal; but the very fact that they bored me admonished me not to sacrifice them—if there was anything to be done with them—simply to irritation. As I look back at this phase they seem to me to have pervaded my life not a little. I have a vision of them as most of the time in my studio, seated, against the wall, on an old velvet bench to be out of the way, and looking like a pair of patient courtiers in a royal ante-chamber. I'm convinced that during the coldest weeks of the winter they held their ground because it saved them fire. Their newness was losing its gloss, and it was impossible not to feel that they were objects of charity. Whenever Miss Churm arrived they went away, and after I was fairly launched in "Rutland Ramsay" Miss Churm arrived pretty often. They managed to express to me tacitly that they supposed I wanted her for the low life of the book, and I let them suppose it, since they had attempted to study the work—it was lying about the studio—without discovering that it dealt only with the highest circles. They had dipped into the most brilliant of our novelists without deciphering many passages. I still took an hour from them, now and again, in spite of Jack Hawley's warning: it would be time enough to dismiss them, if dismissal should be necessary, when the rigor of the season was over. Hawley had made their acquaintance—he had met them at my fireside—and thought them a ridiculous pair. Learning that he was a painter they tried to approach him, to show him too that they were the real thing; but he looked at them, across the big room, as if they were miles away: they were a compendium of everything he most objected to in the social system of his country. Such people as that, all convention and patent-leather, with ejaculations that stopped conversation, had no business in a studio. A studio was a place to learn to see, and how could you see through a pair of feather beds?

The main inconvenience I suffered at their hands was that, at first, I was shy of letting them discover how my artful little servant had begun to sit to me for "Rutland Ramsay." They knew that I had been odd enough (they were prepared by this time to allow oddity to artists) to pick a foreign vagabond out of the streets, when I might have had a person with whiskers and credentials; but it was some time before they learned how high I rated his accomplishments. They found him in an attitude more than once, but they never doubted I was doing him as an organ-grinder. There were several things they never guessed, and one of them was that for a striking scene in the novel, in which a footman briefly figured, it occurred to me to make use of Major Monarch as the menial. I kept putting this off, I didn't like to ask him to don the livery—besides the difficulty of finding a livery to fit him. At last, one day late in the winter, when I was at work on the despised Oronte (he who caught one's idea in an instant), and was in the glow of feeling that I was going very straight, they came in, the Major and his wife, with their society laugh about nothing (there was less and less to laugh at), like country-callers—they always reminded me of that—who have walked across the park after church and are presently persuaded to stay to luncheon. Luncheon was over, but they could stay to tea—I knew they wanted it. The fit was on me, however, and I couldn't let my ardor cool and my work wait, with the fading daylight, while my model prepared it. So I asked Mrs. Monarch if she would mind laying it out—a request which, for an instant, brought all the blood to her face. Her eyes were on her husband's for a second, and some mute telegraphy passed between them. Their folly was over the next instant; his cheerful shrewdness put an end to it. So far from pitying their wounded pride, I must add, I was moved to give it as complete a lesson as I could. They bustled about together and got out the cups and saucers and made the kettle boil. I know they felt as if they were waiting on my servant, and when the tea was prepared I said: "He'll have a cup, please—he's tired." Mrs. Monarch brought him one where he stood, and he took it from her as if he had been a gentleman at a party, squeezing a crush-hat with an elbow.

Then it came over me that she had made a great effort for me—made it with a kind of nobleness—and that I owed her a compensation. Each time I saw her after this I wondered what the compensation could be. I couldn't go on doing the wrong thing to oblige them. Oh, it *was* the wrong thing, the stamp of the work for which they sat—Hawley was not the only person to say it now. I sent in a large number of the drawings I had made for "Rutland Ramsay," and I received a warning that was more to the point than Hawley's. The artistic adviser of the house for which I was working was of opinion that many of my illustrations were not what had been looked for. Most of these illustrations were the subjects in which the Monarchs had figured. Without going into the question of what *had* been looked for, I saw, at this rate I shouldn't get the other books to do. I hurled myself in despair upon Miss Churm, I put her through all her paces. I not only adopted Oronte publicly as my hero, but one morning when the Major looked in to see if I didn't require him to finish a figure for the *Cheapside*, for which he had begun to sit the week before, I told him that I had changed my mind—I would do the drawing from my man. At this my visitor turned pale and stood looking at me. "Is *he* your idea of an English gentleman?" he asked.

I was disappointed, I was nervous, I wanted to get on with my work; so I replied with irritation: "Oh, my dear Major—I can't be ruined for *you!*"

He stood another moment; then without a word, he quitted the studio. I drew a long breath when he was gone, for I said to myself that I shouldn't see him again. I had not told him definitely that I was in danger of having my work rejected, but I was vexed at his not having felt the catastrophe in the air, read with me the moral of our fruitless collaboration, the lesson that, in the deceptive atmosphere of art, even the highest respectability may fail of being plastic.

I didn't owe my friends money, but I did see them again. They reappeared together, three days later, and, under the circumstances, there was something tragic in the fact. It was a proof to me that they could find nothing else in life to do. They had threshed the matter out in a dismal conference— they had digested the bad news that they were not in for the series. If they were not useful to me even for the *Cheapside* their function seemed difficult to determine, and I could only judge at first that they had come, forgivingly, decorously, to take a last leave. This made me rejoice in secret that I had little leisure for a scene; for I had placed both my other models in position together and I was pegging away at a drawing from which I hoped to derive glory. It had been suggested by the passage in which Rutland Ramsay, drawing up a chair to Artemisia's piano-stool, says extraordinary things to her while she ostensibly fingers out a difficult piece of music. I had done Miss Churm at the piano before— it was an attitude in which she knew how to take on an absolutely poetic grace. I wished the two figures to "compose" together, intensely, and my little Italian had entered perfectly into my conception. The pair were vividly before me, the piano had been pulled out; it was a charming picture of blended youth and murmured love, which I had only to catch and keep. My visitors stood and looked at it, and I was friendly to them over my shoulder.

They made no response, but I was used to silent company and went on with my work, only a little disconcerted (even though exhilarated by the sense that *this* was at least the ideal thing), at not having got rid of them after all. Presently I heard Mrs. Monarch's sweet voice beside, or rather above me: "I wish her hair was a little better done." I looked up and she was staring with a strange fixedness at Miss Churm, whose back was turned to her. "Do you mind my just touching it?" she went on—a question which made me spring up for an instant, as with the instinctive fear that she might do the young lady a harm. But she quieted me with a glance I shall never forget—I confess I should like to have been able to paint *that*—and went for a moment to my model. She spoke to her softly, laying a hand on her shoulder and bending over her; and as the girl, understanding, gratefully assented, she disposed her rough curls, with a few quick passes, in such a way as to make Miss Churm's head twice as charming. It was one of the most heroic personal services I've ever seen rendered. Then Mrs. Monarch turned away with a low sigh and, looking about her as if for something to do, stooped to the floor with a noble humility and picked up a dirty rag that had dropped out of my paint-box.

The Major meanwhile had also been looking for something to do and, wandering to the other end of the studio, saw before him my breakfast things, neglected, unremoved. "I say, can't I be useful *here*?" he called out to me with an irrepressible quaver. I assented with a laugh that I fear was awkward and for the next ten minutes, while I worked, I heard the light clatter of china and the tinkle of spoons and glass. Mrs. Monarch assisted her husband—they washed up my crockery, they put it away. They wandered off into my little scullery, and I afterwards found that they had cleaned my knives and that my slender stock of plate had an unprecedented surface. When it came over me, the latent eloquence of what they were doing, I confess that my drawing was blurred for a moment—the picture swam. They had accepted their failure, but they couldn't accept their fate. They had bowed their heads in bewilderment to the perverse and cruel law in virtue of which the real thing could be so much less precious than the unreal; but they didn't want to starve. If my servants were my models, my models might be my servants. They would reverse the parts—the others would sit for the ladies and gentlemen, and *they* would do the work. They would still be in the studio—it was an intense dumb appeal to me not to turn them out. "Take us on," they wanted to say—"we'll do *anything*."

When all this hung before me the *afflatus* vanished—my pencil dropped from my hand. My sitting was spoiled and I got rid of my sitters, who were also evidently rather mystified and awestruck. Then, alone with the Major and his wife, I had a most uncomfortable moment. He put their prayer into a single sentence: "I say, you know—just let *us* do for you, can't you?" I couldn't—it was dreadful to see them emptying my slops; but I pretended I could, to oblige them, for about a week. Then I gave them a sum of money to go away; and I never saw them again. I obtained the remaining books, but my friend Hawley repeats that Major and Mrs. Monarch did me a permanent harm, got me into a second-rate trick. If it be true I am content to have paid the price—for the memory.

The Feminist Press at The City University of New York is a nonprofit institution dedicated to publishing literary and educational works by and about women. We are the oldest continuing feminist publisher in the world; our existence is grounded in the knowledge that many mainstream publishers seeking mass audiences often ignore important, pathbreaking works by women from the United States and throughout the world.

The Feminist Press was founded in 1970. In its early decades the Press launched the contemporary rediscovery of "lost" American women writers, and went on to diversify its list by publishing significant works by American women writers of color. More recently, the Press has added to its roster international women writers who are still far less likely to be translated than male writers. We also seek out nonfiction that explores contemporary issues affecting the lives of women around the world.

The Feminist Press has initiated two groundbreaking long-term projects. Women Writing Africa is an unprecedented four-volume series that documents women's writing in Africa over thousands of years. Funded by the National Science Foundation, The Women Writing Science project celebrates the achievements of women scientists while frankly facing obstacles in their career paths. The Series also promotes scientific literacy among the public at large, and encourages young women to choose careers in science.

Founded in an activist spirit, The Feminist Press is currently undertaking initiatives that will bring its books and educational resources to underserved populations, including community colleges, public high schools, literacy and ESL programs, and international libraries. As we move forward into the twenty-first century, we continue to expand our work to respond to women's silences wherever they are found.

For information about events and for a complete catalog of the Press's more than 300 books, please refer to our website: www. feministpress.org or call (212) 817-7915 to request a catalog with our entire list.